AF392821

Cave

A science fiction novel

Richard G. Hole

Science Fiction and Fantasy

Any attempt to rebel was punishable by death.

Trying to bring down the apathy, employing a more
or less manual job to shake it off, however slight,
was the last pain.

The disintegrators.

There the bodies would stop, of which there was not
even the slightest trace ...

**Cave** is a story belonging to the Science Fiction series, a collection of science fiction and fantasy novels

# CAVE

CHAPTER I

He hated all this.
He hated Kronos, and he hated Alvia too.
Alvia was tall, beautiful, and black-eyed.
Alvia was programmed to love, to bear children, to live with someone like him, or better than him.
Everything was programmed on the Planet.
That's why he hated Kronos.
That's why he hated Alvia.
They both lived ... vegetated, slept or loved, but nothing more. That was what his Science had become.
It was not like this in the past.
Kelf remembered.
Three, four or five thousand years ago, it was not that way.
What about their cells?
What about the biochemical makeup of your body?
Hated it too?
Yes, there was also no other answer than that.
Alvia was white-skinned and rosy, Alvia was smart, the smartest in the Galaxy I.
A lot, but not enough to get inside his magnetic computer brain.
There was only someone who surpassed it, Kronos himself.
So he had to be careful.
The Being-Robot, or the Robot-Being.
That was the unknown.
A scientist with more than five thousand years of existence, who could move from here to there, at his free will, at his free will, but whose movements were automaton because everything was controlled.
Even the ability to love or hate.
Only hatred, if any, was beyond Kronos's will.
A will that was undoing the Planet.
"Robots", mutants, machines everywhere.
They loved, drank, went to the so-called cinema or theater ..., with performances and films controlled to the fifth of a second.
One hour to start and another to finish.
Program for lunch, dinner or sleep.
Empty fields, and full of robot machines.

They did and unmade as they pleased, sowing, harvesting crops, without a single failure.
Even the water in the clouds was controlled.
The rest, the beings of the planet, vegetated in the armchairs in the sun, on the beaches, under the trees, loving, caressing, kissing ..., but nothing more.
Time for love, to sleep, to wake up ... and to go for walks, long walks, tireless walks, and then go to lie down anywhere.
Like Frida and Volmen.
From there, I could see them.
Next to the fountain of the Great Central Plaza, in the shade, closely embraced ... Beings who were used for nothing more than to enjoy.
But what did they enjoy?
No problem.
They were ... unreal, even though their shadows were cast on the ground.
They had no feelings, no ideas of their own, because Kronos had seized them.
Exactly how it happened to him.
"Kelf, you have to do this or that" and he did.
"Alvia is very lonely tonight, go see her, Kelf," and he had to.
Hours to love, to enjoy, to laugh or sing; but all under an express order.
The Planet was invaded by the apathy of the beings that populated it, and Kronos had been the main architect, although he also had part of the fault that this happened.
Perhaps the oldest.
Alvia knew how to love, but her love was controlled, and Kelf didn't want that.
The Being-Robot or the Robo-Being.
It was ... the usual unknown, which jumped into his mind second by second, as soon as he was faced with one of those mutants.
But actually, there, on the Planet, who was the Mutant, the Robot?
The beings that populated it, like him and Alvia, or were they called Robots, who ruled everything, ruling their lives and minds?
Any attempt to rebel was punishable by death.
Trying to bring down the apathy, employing a more or less manual job to shake it off, however slight, was the last pain.
The disintegrators.
There the bodies would stop, of which there was not even the slightest trace.
That's why he hated Kronos, and why he hated himself.
Alvia could have children.
The Great Doctors of the Planet had told her when she went to live with him, but Alvia didn't want them.

He did not like the slow process or the inconvenience it would undoubtedly cause him.
That's why he hated Alvia.
Exchange her for another, for another being of a different sex to live with him?
He could, of course, but in his report to the President, he should give certain data, which he preferred to keep to himself.
Frida and Volmen had sat with their backs leaning against the retaining wall of the Great Central Fountain.
They looked into each other's eyes.
Kelf checked his watch.
They had exactly four minutes and thirty seconds left, then they would get up from there and, arm in arm, begin to walk away, taking the "usual" walk under the trees of the park.
Kelf knew that if they lingered for a split second longer than necessary, a Robot-Being would send them a warning.
The third, if it came, would be punished and, later, if the act was repeated ...
"What are you looking at, Kelf?
Slowly, he turned away from the window, turned, and faced her.
Alvia was beautiful and had skin ...
Tall, with firm breasts, or its equivalent, and her legs fully exposed, she was perfect, or at least Kelf thought so.
I was smiling at him.
"To Frida and Volmen" he answered, cutting off the train of his thoughts; closing his mind to hers, afraid that she might guess what her thoughts were about Kronos, about the future, and about herself. " They are at the source.
"Someday they will make a mistake" he paused, and approached him, putting his hands on his shoulders, while Kelf's went to his waist, pulling her against his chest in an almost irresistible way, and added ": When will you take me? under the trees, Kelf? They all do it one day or another, and you and I live together.
"But you don't want children.
"I hate them.
And kissed him, in contrast to his words.
Kelf said nothing.
His lips parted on hers, and he returned Alvia's caress gently. Then he separated her from his arms.
"Kronos wants to see you, Kelf" she said, as soon as she had.
"For what?
"Kronos never gives an explanation. He commands and we obey.

"Yes I know. And you...?
"I'll wait" she looked at him thoughtfully and added, after a couple or three seconds of silence, "I think for a few hours, we are going to get out of control.
"And you don't like that, do you?
"Do not.
"Why?
"You try to force me, when this happens. Time no longer counts for you, when it comes to me.
"And you don't want children?
"You know that, Kelf" she replied. Therefore, why always ask the same thing?
Kelf smiled.
White, rosy, amber skin ...
"I could force you. A complaint to Kronos ...
She approached him, undulating.
"You won't do that, Kelf" she whispered, her hands already on his neck, her lips tickling him. You will not do it.
"Why? Kelf repeated like an automaton.
Alvia stopped kissing him, took a step back and replied
"You love me…, and that loses you, dear. Come on, go, and don't make him wait. Kronos would be upset.
Kelf knew it was true.
It didn't bother him, not a little, not too much, but he didn't want that to happen, not for the moment.
He turned and, without answering, approached one of the walls; the panel slid back on its own, and in front of him, leaving enough space for him to enter.
He did so, and silently on its invisible rails, it closed behind him, and Kelf saw himself where he had seen himself countless times.
The Great Central Ship of Kronos.
Long and wide, immeasurable, with its own light that seemed to come from everywhere, and at the same time from nowhere.
Double row of mutants, of Robots-Beings, silent, manipulating the complicated mechanism of the ship.
Buttons, red and white, innumerable, as infinite as the number itself, screens that turned on that went off, running on wheels, gears, tape recorders, but in silence, in silence from beyond the grave.
He began to advance among the Robots-Beings who turned to look at him as silent as the machine itself, and he approached the general control panel and, with the expert's hand, began to manipulate.

In front of him the television screen lit up and he asked:
"Have you called me?
And the answer was:
"You are fifteen seconds and three tenths late, Kelf, and I don't like that.
"Yes I know. Sorry, it won't happen again.
But he was lying, and that, Kronos didn't know.
"Was it Alvia?
"No, it wasn't her. I delayed myself.
"You are lying, Kelf! It was Alvia.
Kronos knew it.
Kelf stiffened, wondering if he didn't know everything else as well, everything he thought of the Planet System.
"Yes, it was her" he replied, more than anything to break that silence that could still seem much more suspicious than if he continued speaking.
"Good. . Alvia, Kelf. It will give you children.
He did not want to contradict him, and replied with a single word, which in turn was quite a question:
"Y...?
Kronos was slow to answer.
"Something is wrong, Kelf.
His muscles tensed like steel cables.
"What is not working...?
"Something inside me is failing.
He frowned.
"Explain yourself, will you?
"Something inside my mind, you understand? Ideas that want to penetrate it and that they cannot. This never happened, and you know it.
"And good...?
"Tonight you will have to come here. May Alvia accompany you.
"For what?
"You have to check everything. The circuits, the alarms and ... everything.
"Can I do it alone?
"Alvia will accompany you, Kelf. It is my wish. I want to see her next to you.
"It's okay. Alvia will accompany me "he repeated like an automaton.
"That's fine, Kelf.
He did not answer for the moment, he just took a long look at the double row of Robots-Beings and, already looking at Kronos again, he inquired:
"They will stay to help me, right?
"You will do it by yourself, Kelf. I don't want anyone else, prying inside the machine, the circuits, the computers, the ...

Kelf pretended to listen to him, but he wasn't.
Thought.
Tonight he could.
There would be no other occasion, for a long time.
": ... and now that you know what I want, go away, Kelf. Alvia is waiting for you. She is eager to take you home.
Did not answer; had he done so, he would surely have burst out laughing.
He was a creator and he was going to destroy.
That was all.
In front of his eyes, the screen went black, and then, without a single hesitation, Kelf turned and started toward the exit.

CHAPTER II

It was coming from the kitchen or its equivalent, and it was approaching him, smiling, fascinating, aware of its power over beings of the opposite sex.
About the Beings-Robots, like her and like himself.
Kelf knew what was going to happen next.
Exactly like other times.
The white, semi-metallic skirt and the long, perfect, naked legs.
She kept looking at him, continuing to smile at him desirable, as if giving or rejecting. Of that of that last Kelf, he was never sure.
He struggles with himself, not to get up and run to her to clasp her in his arms, but to not look at the two glasses that were next to him, on the table.
"I'm done, Kelf.
She was very close to him when he did so and he reached out one of his hands and took it in his.
Alvia sat on his legs and they kissed.
"Do you love me, Kelf?
"Yes, and you?
"Too.
He stroked one of her bare legs.
"However ..." he began,
Alvia cut him short, frowning.
"Are we going to get back to the same thing, Kelf? "I ask.
And there was disgust in his voice.
"Tonight" he replied, "we will go to see Kronos.
"Yes, I know" replied Alvia, with perfect calm ", but you will not tell him. You can not.
"You are very sure.
He saw her smile, and then his question surprised him:
"How old are you, Kelf?
Looking at her in amazement, he replied:
"Millennials, Alvia, and I'm not lying to you.
"I know. That is where we are not alike. Your biological makeup is different from mine.
"What do you mean?
"When I am an old woman full of wrinkles, unrecognizable, you will continue in the same way. You are not mortal, Kelf.
"Is it a reason?
"Is one of them. The others I already explained to you.
"Is not sufficient.

"There are those millennia ... that have been of no use to you, if you don't know what I mean" he hesitated a little, without Kelf saying anything and, suddenly, he threw his arms around his neck ": Oh , Kelf! I love you ... I love you so much you know In spite of everything ...

Alvia herself broke off as she pressed her lips against those others who at first seemed cold to her and who suddenly took on sudden heat, as she felt held by the powerful arms that enervated her.

When they parted, it had been more than a long minute, and it was still several more seconds before Kelf reacted, loving them both, while she kept one of her rosy, shapely arms around his neck.

"Here, Alvia" he said, offering her one. We are going to drink, and immediately we go.

He took it, smiling.

"For you, Kelf" he said for a second before raising it to his lips.

She drank, and Kelf coolly imitated her.

There was a second of waiting, maybe two, and suddenly, Alvia's head tilted to one side, and the man held her so she wouldn't fall to the ground.

And with her in his arms, and he approached the bedroom, laid her softly on the bed, turned around and reached the threshold of the door.

He didn't look at her.

He hated her and at that moment the Planet, the planet's fate, her future destiny, mattered much more than Alvia.

When he woke up the next day, he would find CHAOS.

The Robots-Beings would be on the ground, as what they were, dolls of metal, steel or their equivalent, broken, disarticulated, lifeless ... that would no longer return to them because Kronos would have died.

The dreadful CHAOS.

Civilization destroyed ... but that civilization, and not the Robots-Beings.

They would live, they would have to think, to fend for themselves by their own means, and the Planet, slowly, in decades, in long decades, regain its freshness, the working life that it already had millennia ago.

Of freshness and of life, and not of slow death, as was the case at that time. Without laziness, without apathy, and without so many things that were slowly consuming him.

He would recover. I would come out of CHAOS.

Of that, Kelf was completely sure.

He left the bedroom and began to cross to the other side of the great room, toward the door that led to the street.

It did not arrive.

A low buzz, but long and monotonous, brought him to a halt, as if he had suddenly taken root in the ground.

Kronos!

He looked at his watch.

No, it could not be Kronos who was calling him at that hour, since there was no delay in his departure.

Everything had been measured, controlled to the thousandth of a second.

No, of course, it wasn't Kronos.

Then who?

The buzzing persisted, and Kelf knew it wouldn't stop until he lifted the kind of handset, hidden behind a small panel on the wall.

He strode over, pulled it back, and pressed one of the buttons.

In front of his eyes, a red light flashed rapidly, and then it was fixed, and almost immediately, he heard the voice.

Unrecognizable, scratchy, a little hoarse, but nonetheless had familiar undertones.

"Kelf ...?

"Yes. Who are you?

"It does not matter now. Listen to me, please "there was anguish in the voice, an infinite anguish." Don't do it, you understand?

"What is it that I don't have to do?

"Don't do it until I go. Please ... it would be horrible for you. Very horrible. Something that he would never forget. Do not do it. Respond.

Kelf, frowning and a little nervous, asked him:

"Where are you?

"It's long distance" seemed to drown. On the other continent. He spoke to her from there. Please, Kelf, don't do that tonight.

Again he hesitated.

A crazy?

It could be or maybe not.

In doubt Kelf replied: I am not trying to do ...

The voice from the other side interrupted him:

"I'm going to take a rocket plane, you understand? I'll be there in about seven or eight hours and we'll talk. I ... I can't and don't want to explain it to you by this means, you wouldn't believe me.

The red lightbulb in front of his eyes went out, and Kelf realized that he had cut off the communication.

He closed the panel and turned to look at the bedroom door.

Alvia continued to sleep, she would continue that way until well into the next day ... and maybe ... maybe they would never see each other again.

At least, no, within that state of affairs.

A crazy?

He shrugged, and once again looked at his watch.

He would have to hurry.

He went out into the street, fully armed.

No one would register you

As the Great Scientist of the Planet, he had the full confidence of the President and Kronos himself.

Kronos ... the one he wanted to destroy, the one he was going to destroy that very night, and it was paradoxical.

He stepped onto the wide sidewalk, and instantly a robot car pulled up beside him, and the door corresponding to that side opened to let him into the vehicle.

Kelf did, settled into the back seat, and the cold, metallic voice of the machine asked:

"Where is Alvia, Kelf? Kronos told me she was coming with you too.

Kelf smiled.

"Dinner was bad for him, and he can't do it. Kronos himself will call the doctor.

"Kronos is not going to like that.

"I know," Kelf replied with perfect calm. You take me?

There was no answer, but the machine started towards Planet Headquarters. The Great Central Fountain, now illuminated, and Kelf, seeing it, thought of Volmen and Frida.

Maybe they would be glad about what he was going to do tonight.

He got out of the robot car in front of the Great Gate and, with his eyes fixed on the six robots that formed the guard, began to climb the steps, white and gleaming, shiny, of a prefabricated material expressly for that purpose.

Robots-Beings who respectfully made way for him, saying "good night" to him with their equal, programmed, metallic and cold voices of living machines.

Robots-Beings that that night would end their guard in a way very different from the usual, since at that time the Being-Robot would have reached the culmination of a fact, to regain the Being, within the Planet.

He crossed the door, replying to "good night" and, without turning his head once, also without a single hesitation, he walked towards the room where he was with Alvia that afternoon, and then, straight to the panel that was pulled back to one side to give way.

Four seconds later, Kelf found himself facing Kronos.

The empty room, without a soul.

Without a sound, even though its thousands of mechanisms continued to work with solar precision.

"You have arrived on time, Kelf" was what he said for all greetings. And Alvia?

"Dinner was bad for him and he couldn't come.
There was a silence, which seemed long and heavy, which made her nervous.
Kronos broke it after that time, with a new question:
"Can you do it yourself?
Smiled.
"This is not the first time" he said.
"Yes, I know, but Alvia… I like to see her around here. Alvia is beautiful, Kelf, and no one knows it better than you "and he added, abruptly," Where are you going to start?
"By the alarm circuits.
"Later…?
"The extra sensory ones, and if I can't find the fault, I'll have to dig into your mind.
"I know.
"Then…
A new silence followed, but this one was much shorter than the previous one.
Kronos cut it, the same as always:
"Move over, Kelf. I am looking forward to getting this over with. It's as if my insides wanted to warn me of something, and I couldn't … and I don't like that feeling.
Kelf stepped back a little, and his gaze swept through the entire facility, the entire automated complex.
With eyes of what he was, of an expert.
Finally, Kelf began to walk toward the bottom of the Great Ship.
He was almost there, when the alarm began to sound.
Soft first, louder later, and then its sound spread through Planet First City, shaking it to its foundations.
He turned just as Kronos's sarcastic laugh reached his ears, and his words:
"You are going to die, Kelf. Surrender without resistance.
The long ship in front of him, fully lit, silent as ever, the thousands of gears turning and turning… and bulbs that go out, that light up, but empty.
Kelf did not hesitate.
With the weapon in hand, a strange looking flat weapon, small, but powerful, since its effects were devastating, he ran towards the exit.
Kronos's laugh went deep into him, just as the panel slid to one side to let him pass and it closed in the same way, behind him, as soon as he had.
The corridor.
Silent, gloomy despite being as illuminated as the ship he had just left.
The bend.

Kelf kept running.

The Great Gate.

The exit.

There the six Robots-Beings would be waiting for him, with the express order to kill him.

He kept running to a stop before he got there, panting, sweaty, his lungs about to burst out of his mouth.

He opened it like a fish out of water.

He was trapped.

Kronos had known everything from the beginning, and it was at that moment, reaching that conclusion, that he remembered the call from that night.

Who...?

Why didn't you pay attention?

Around him, the silence was more threatening than the ghostly laughter of Kronos and the presence of all the Robot-Guardians of the Great House, and of the Planet.

He thought of Alvia.

Alvia, who would be sleeping, victim of the drug that he gave her, mixed with the glass of liquor.

He hated Alvia.

He meditated on her, on that call, hesitating between going out or staying in there until the Great Door opened to give them way, pistol in hand at hip level.

Until he made a sudden decision.

CHAPTER III

His heart had stopped beating with that terrifying force that made him stop with his back against the wall.

It was the moment.

Kelf stepped away, glanced back down the corridor behind him, to the bend that hid everything else from his view.

Slowly, he began to walk.

He was making the Great Gate, noticing how, once again, and that now he was not running, his forehead began to perspire.

One step, two, three, even four, not placing himself in the center of the corridor, but brushing against the wall to his left, and suddenly, as if obeying a silent order, the Great Door opened, and then he saw, some seconds before they saw him and he didn't hesitate.

Pulled the trigger.

There was a faint sound, and two of the Robot-Beings went up in smoke, after a blue flash that nearly blinded him.

Kelf threw himself to the ground, as the other four fired bolts at him.

The wall behind his back made a click, and a cloud of rubble fell the length and breadth of it, as he rolled over on himself, and the voice of Kronos was heard throughout the planet:

"I want him alive, you assholes. Adjust your weapons.

It was a mistake.

Kelf understood it that way.

An error of a thousandth of a second, but he understood it in much less time, in something infinitely smaller, and he acted just as the four of them raised their weapons, not to disintegrate him, turning him to dust, but adjusting them so as not to kill him.

One of those rays struck his body, he would fall to the ground, deprived of knowledge, and what would come later would possibly be much worse than death itself.

He did not let them.

For four consecutive times, he sent the rays, and the penetrating and unpleasant smell of burned cables and circuits, reached his nostrils at the precise moment that writhing on the ground, between sparks of fire, he disappeared from his sight.

The Great Gate was open in front of him.

Kelf ran there.

The street.

He descended the steps, looking around, as the alarm sounded again, telling the inhabitants of the Great City that a Robot-Being had escaped from Kronos.
I was alone.
He couldn't even go home to Alvia, despite his hatred for her.
That would be where they would first look for him.
Perhaps they were already next to her, waiting for him.
Kronos would have anticipated everything, even in the event that he might escape from the Great House.
He reached the corner.
Only.
He was completely alone in the Big City.
No one would open a single door or reach out to help him, knowing what that would mean to him who did.
He started walking, fingers clenched on the gun, looking for an exit in the direction of the extreme neighborhoods.
Frida and Volmen.
Them neither.
Alone, completely alone.
Kronos just had to wait a little longer to hunt him down.
Very little else.
Above his head, the blackness of the sky, and the stars in their inexorable march in the Universe.
Below, the Great City and the death trap it now represented for him.
Kelf came to the corner.
He bent it, and as he did so, he saw them.
Two, who separated from each other as soon as they saw him, and just as he was diving headfirst to the ground.
The lightning passed very close to his body, crashed against the wall of the house behind him, without producing the slightest sound or leaving the slightest trace, so he understood, without any effort, that the order of Kronos, with Regarding that he wanted him alive, he had reached all the Guardians of the Planet.
He fired, twice, after jumping towards one of the portals, and the flare of both illuminated the entire gloomy alley where he was at that moment.
Kelf started running.
Frida and ...
He didn't complete the thought because at that moment he saw her, on the sidewalk, running toward him with the long head of hair fluttering behind her.

Frida was also a brunette, and her eyes were large and slanted, brown, very dark.
Frida was also beautiful and he liked her, but he couldn't mix her in that.
"Come" he said, barely reaching his side "; come on, come with me.
He was grabbing his hand, pulling him.
He resisted.
"I can't go with you, Frida" he said.
"Come" she repeated. I'm going to take you to a safe place.
"I can not. I don't want you to ... On the other hand, I can't go to your house. They would look for me there, and Volmen wouldn't like it. And Kronos.
He would end up with you the same as
Frida interrupted him:
"Volmen doesn't count in this, Kelf.
"But...
"We live, but nothing more. I don't love him, and he knows it. Kronos commands, and we obey, but nothing more,
He tugged on his hand again, and Kelf made a gesture of resignation.
A safe place, that was what he needed, and Frida had promised it.
He began to walk, without her letting him go, and in a few minutes he knew that he was taking him home, to the dwelling he shared with Volmen.
"Frida ...
"Yes? And she cocked her beautiful brown head to look at him.
"Volmen won't let me in.
"He is not at home. It won't come all night.
"Even so, the Robot-Beings ...
"They won't find you. You and I will go, as I told you, to a safe place. You won't be in the house for long. Just a few minutes. Come on, Kelf, I'm not cheating on you "he paused, still walking, without letting go of his hand and asked": And Alvia?
"Sleep.
"How is it possible...?
"I'll tell you about it later.
Home.
It was a few minutes after he finished speaking that Kelf found himself in front of his door.
Beside him, Frida released his hand, took a few steps forward, and opened the door.
"Come in, Kelf" he said in a whisper.
He crossed the threshold.
And he didn't even notice the places she led him until he stopped in the center of his own bedroom.

"Wait for me here, Kelf.

"Where are you going?

He smiled at her.

His teeth were perfect.

A trifle thing, to look at that and under such circumstances, but Kelf did it that way.

"Looking for food, Kelf. We may have to stay together for a while.

It was the obligatory question, and he asked it:

"And Volmen?

"It does not count in this. I'll tell you outside.

He didn't wait for an answer, he turned around and saw her disappear into one of the rooms.

It took a few minutes to return, and it came fully loaded with packages.

"Help me, Kelf" he asked.

And he did.

When she finished, Frida bent down, pushed aside the carpet that was on the floor and could see the hatch, which she then raised.

A stair.

"You come down first.

He began to do so without answering, without asking anything, and she followed suit, closing it next.

Darkness.

Kelf began to feel the steps, just as Frida shone a flashlight on them.

A runner.

Kelf continued on, feeling her by his side, the graceful click of her shoes on the hard floor and, more than anything else in itself, her feminine presence, and everything she represented to him, at any given moment.

Hours

Kelf never knew, but suddenly the corridor ended, closing in front of his eyes with what appeared to be live rock.

He turned to look at her.

Frida was smiling at him.

"There is a way out.

"Yes...?

"Kronos doesn't know, but I'm sure they'll find this passage, only when they do, we won't be here.

She approached the wall, her back to him, and for the first time since she had been tripped over that night, Kelf's eyes went to her magnificent legs, which were almost completely exposed by the very short skirt.

A buzz.

He was startled, and stopped looking at her to, in a completely mechanical way, turn his eyes to the rock that blocked his path.
It was rushing to the side, as was the panel behind which Kronos was hiding.
"Come on, Kelf" she said, breaking her thoughts into a thousand pieces. You have to cross to the other side, or it will close again and now ... we won't be able to open until a few hours later. Runs!
He did, taking her by the hand, pulling her as he had before.
The other side.
I look.
Rocks, sharp edges, bushes, trees, the moon, the stars, the mountain.
I ask:
Where is the Big City?
Frida laughed.
"Behind this very mountain, Kelf" replied. And don't stop, we can't stay here, for long.
He did not respond and began to walk, leading her, as always, to his side.
A path between the rocks.
"I discovered it by chance," she explained.
“With Volmen?
"Alone. A pleasure to take walks that Kronos does not control. And trust me, Kelf, most of the inhabitants of the Big City do.
"Why don't they rebel?
“They are afraid of dying. Like me, like yourself ... and also like Kronos. The more than any of us. That is why he does not let anyone get close to him. It is their triumph against yours, Kelf. Against the Being that ...
"Drop that, will you?
"Yes, of course, I did not want to bother you. We are going?
"Yes.
They walked on along the rocky path, leaving no trace of their passing, until it came to an abrupt end, round a bend, and Kelf found himself facing the granite and basalt masses of the mountain.
He looked back.
In the distance, it seemed to him to distinguish the clarities of a new day.
"It will be dawn soon, Frida" she commented, wanting to break the silence that surrounded them in any way.
She did not answer
Again she had turned her back to him, manipulating the shadow of her splendid body of being young and beautiful, and the buzzing was repeated.
The rock moved in front of his eyes.
The hole, big, almost as much or more than the Great Door of the Headquarters of the President of the Planet and of Kronos.

And Frida's small, well-cared hand between hers
"Come in, Kelf" invited ", here we will be safe.
He thought of Volmen, but did not speak his name, no longer wishing to do so.
They entered, walking illuminated by the kind of deaf lantern that Frida was carrying in her hands and Kelf could see above her head at an enormous height in some places, the stalactites on the ceiling, which told her about the past.
From a married of centuries.
They continued descending towards the bowels of the Planet until, also in a sudden abrupt way, the descent was finished.
The grotto.
There it formed a kind of grandiose plaza, and around it, several more mouths, at the entrance to as many caves.
"We can go into that one, Kelf" she said. It will be enough for both of us.
"Did not answer.
They crossed to the other side, silently, entered, and the light shone.
Kelf looked at her in amazement.
"I've been installing all of this for months, Kelf.
"For what?
"Like a retreat.
"For you?
"Yes.
I couldn't see his face.
He was dropping the packages on the ground, and Kelf, waiting for the answer, followed suit.
"Alone?
"Do not.
"With another Being of a different sex?
"Yes. A getaway ... with you, Kelf. Always want it. I love you, you know?
It was that simple, finishing placing the last packages on the rock floor.
Then he straightened up, and they were face to face, very close to each other, almost touching.
"Can I believe it, Frida?
"Oh, Kelf… what… what a beautiful madness…!
And she threw herself into his arms, seeking her lips with a fire that threatened to consume everything.
At least that was the feeling Kelf experienced as he began to reciprocate her touch.
Then much later, with her head resting on her bare thighs, while she sat on the ground with her back against the rock, Kelf closed her eyes.

He was very tired, enormously tired.
Fell asleep.
On her face, Frida's sensual red lips smiled as her eyes shone with unusual strength.
He had held in his arms Kelf, the man for whom he began to hate Alvia, and who was now sleeping like a child, completely trusting in her.
And he liked the feeling he was experiencing.

# CHAPTER IV

He opened his eyes.

His head rested on the girl's tight thighs, and she was dozing, hers leaning against the wall.

Kelf began to move gently, not wanting to wake her, not even wondering how this had happened between the two of them.

He sat down on the floor, and instantly saw himself in front of Frida's eyes, who was looking at him with a bit of a start.

"Kelf ..." he exclaimed, "Oh, Kelf! Don't go, I don't want you to go, do you understand? Nor do I want to be killed.

He linked his arms around her neck, and kissed her once more.

"I'm not going to leave" he said.

She released him.

"Really?

-That's right "he answered", but one day or another I'll have to do it.

"Do not!

It was almost a scream, but Kelf pretended not to have heard it.

"I have to do it, you understand?

And you will die. Your body will disappear without leaving ...

"It can happen, Frida; I know that too, but I love Kronos, and I'm going to finish him off.

"I know all that, Frida, and because I know, I want to.

"You ... you ...

She rose to her feet, and Kelf followed suit.

"You are the first one I truly love. Do you get it?

"Yes.

"Well, understand also that I don't want to lose you.

"None of that is going to happen, but I have to get out.

"Now?

"No." He looked at his watch.

Ten, seven seconds and four tenths.

Kronos had arranged it that way too, down to the millisecond.

Day or night?

Kelf asked himself the question, when she was already answering:

"Listen, Kelf" he said; I want to stay with you. Live with you. Kronos assigned you to another woman ...

"I know.

"You love her?

"Do not.

"Me neither Volmen. And that's another of the things I told you too. And now what are you going to do?
"Get out, Frida, but not now.
"Is there no other way to ...?
"No, there is not.
Closer still, so much that Kelf felt the heat of her body against his, Frida replied:
"I will do.
"That...?
"Listen, Kelf, I am going out shortly, and you will wait for me.
"For what?
"Volmen, among other things. I don't want you to start looking for me, and to bring this to the attention of Kronos. If he does, he will relate us, one way or another.
"It will happen.
"I know, but by then, it may be too late.
"Apart from Volmen, Frida, what are you planning to do?
"Try to know things, Kelf. Things that may be important to you.
"That would be dangerous" he looked at her from head to toe, and added ": On the other hand, after what happened between us, I do not want you to return to Volmen.
"He won't have me, Kelf, you can be sure. We all know how to do things in a way that ... that ... He won't realize it, but I won't be his again. It is a promise.
"When will you do it?
"I'm hungry" she replied, more prosaic than Kelf "Therefore, not before lunch or dinner. I have lost, with the dream, the notion of time.
He prepared the food, cold, which they devoured in silence.
When he finished, Frida stood up,
"What time is it? "I ask.
"Half past eleven.
She drew closer to the mouth of the cave, and Kelf followed her.
"You will come back...?
She turned to look at him.
He was smiling at her.
"Do you expect otherwise? He asked, in turn.
"I do not know.
Did not answer.
I mean, he didn't do that, but he did say:
"Come, I'll show you the springs.
Kelf followed her.

Half an hour later, he was gone.
He consulted his watch as the great mass of rock closed behind him, and he retraced his steps.
I had to think.
Kronos, the launch pads; but I couldn't do it, not without help.
Frida ...
I remembered.
Hour after hour, until a moment came when he himself had to prepare something to eat, which he devoured materially.
Then hour after hour; twenty in all.
Frida ... that she did not return, that perhaps she would not return anymore
He had to get out of there, and try again.
Volmen ... Well, Volmen wouldn't help him, no one would, in the Big City.
Twenty hours, during which time Kelf scanned the grotto inch by inch, meditating, becoming familiar with it, perhaps for further exploration.
A rumor.
The weapon he kept appeared in his hand, and he went to hide behind the stalactites that, like mushrooms, seemed to grow behind his back.
He waited, and it was very little.

* * *


He was carrying several packages when he saw her enter.
"Where have you been?
Frida looked at him, smiling at him. He took a few steps forward, wriggled out of their hands, and walked over to the table, where he released them.
"I asked you a question.
I heard you "he turned to look at him." You have not seen him? "He said-.
I went out to buy some things "he paused slightly and, as he approached her, he asked a new question": When have you returned?
Volmen's hands were on his waist, when he replied:
"Soon, like I told you. A little getaway ...
"That Kronos isn't going to like it, when he finds out.
"Are you going to tell him? Come on, go, in the street there are robot-Guardians. It is materially full.
"You are jealous, and that is not right, Volmen. That feeling should not count, neither for you nor for anyone, or it is programmed.
"Yes I know.
He was leaning on her lips.
Frida put her head forward and offered hers, but broke the embrace, laughing, as soon as Volmen's hands began to press on her waist.

"Now, Volmen, I have a job. All this has to be fixed.
"Where have you been? He said, as if he hadn't heard her.
"Shopping
"You already told me that.
And is it not true?
"To go shopping, you had to get up very early, Frida.
"Why do you think it this way?
"I arrived with the light of the new day, and you were not in bed.
"I got out, the same as you. A little getaway. You know I do, sometimes.
"Alone?
He showed her teeth in a smile.
"Do not.
"A being other than you?
"Yes, but nothing will happen. Just accompany me. We went to the great esplanade. He is a foreigner, and he wanted to see her, to know her.
"And accompanied by another Being, biologically different from its own biochemical composition?
"And why not? Alvia is beautiful, Volmen
"What do you mean?
Frida approached him.
"Nothing, that you do not know" she held out her arms, and allowed herself to be clasped by those others who wanted her but nothing more, and then she separated from them and said ": I was joking.
And lying.
Frida arched an eyebrow.
How are you so sure that I lie, that I have lied to you? "He laughed, and added" I was completely alone, Volmen. I wanted to be, do you understand? Sometimes it happens to me.
A new question was imposed, and Frida asked it after a few seconds of silence:
"And you?
"I confess that I could not come before.
"Why?
"But ..." he looked at her, hesitantly, and added ": Have you not found out yet?
He sat down, still watching her closely.
"You mean Kelf?
"Yes.
"There is I don't know what in the street… I saw the Robots-Guardians, and I didn't want to make any more inquiries. All the inhabitants of the Big City know that Kelf is your friend.

"It was.
"Not anymore?
"Do not. He wanted to destroy Kronos, and Kronos gives us everything. Even the air we breathe.
"And love...?
"Also love, Frida. Like he gave it to Kelf, like he gave it to me. One word was enough to get you.
"Not counting on me, right?
"You don't count, in that sense. Your obligation comes down to one: have children.
"There are many more, Volmen.
"That are unimportant.
Frida was silent, not wanting to continue on that terrain, but broke it after a brief silence with a request that, judging by her tone, only meant the curiosity she might feel about a fact already accomplished.
"And Alvia?
"In the Great House.
"What did he go there for?
"This morning they found her asleep, and they took her away.
"Are they going to ...?
"Kronos said no, Frida. She had to accompany Kelf to the Great House last night, and Kelf drugged her to go completely alone. As you can see, she is not guilty.
"How ... how ...?
"Kronos knows everything. It is necessary Kelf received a call last night, from the other Continent, and the operator relayed it to the Great House. They were waiting for him, and he escaped. Now they are looking for him.
"Do you think they will find him?
"You do not?
Frida looked at him tightly, before answering:
"I simply asked you a question, Volmen.
"Yes, it is true" he looked at her, hesitantly, and added in a thoughtful tone: "Today we will not be able to lie down under the shadow of the Central Fountain. Frida, or walk under the trees.
"Why? It is almost time.
"Forget this. Kronos said to go see the President.
"Your! "And there was amazement in his voice." For what?
"I don't know. The President gives an order, and you have to obey.
"Yes, they rule and we limit ourselves ...
"Frida!
"Yes !?

“I don't like it when you express yourself that way.
"Sorry, Volmen, it won't happen again.
“You always say that.
“Now I will keep my word.
And he was thinking of Kelf, in Kelf's arms when he gave her the answer.
He did not answer that, but he did specify:
"Make me food. I have just the time.
“To go to the Great House?
"Yes that's how it is.
Now, the one who didn't answer was Frida.
Kelf's arms, Kelf's caresses, Kelf's kisses.
Frida turned and left him alone, and did not return to his side until the noon meal had been prepared.
He sat down with Volmen.
Another thing, it would have been suspicious.
They ate with appetite, their eyes on the clock on the mantel, counting the minutes they had to take to do so, both silent.
When he finished, Volmen rose to his feet, and she followed suit.
"Are you leaving already?
The question was unnecessary, since she already knew it, but Frida, for want of something better, asked it.
Volmen was walking around the table, approaching her when he replied:
“They are waiting for me, Frida.
He grasped her by the shoulders, and then slid his large, strong hands down to her waist, while his agate eyes gazed at her with complacency.
He was leaning ...
Frida kissed him, accepting and returning the caress, and then accompanied him to the door.
"When will you return?
"I do not know
"Tonight...?
“I don't know, Frida. That will depend on the President and perhaps the Grand Council.
"Is there a meeting?
"Yes.
“But you don't belong to the ...
"I know" he interrupted, "but I have to go. Kronos wants it.
“Kronos and always Kronos, and the President.
Frida thought so, but what she said was:
“I will wait for you all night.
Volmen did not respond, and went out into the street.

Frida closed the door behind him, and he began to cross it diagonally, taking advantage of his free passage to do so with his eyes fixed on the Robots-Guardians who in turn observed his apparently calm march towards the Great House, and then They returned their attention to the street and the house where Frida was completely alone.

The Esplanade, the Fountain, the shadow under which he had hugged and kissed Frida ... and the steps that gave access to the Great Door.

And six Robots standing guard.

But they were different from the ones Kelf disintegrated.

He started up the stairs, noticing how two of them came forward to meet him.

Volmen didn't stop.

His tall, strong Nordic stature seemed to dominate them all, for brief seconds, but it was nothing more than that, an illusion of his own senses.

The stairway was behind.

They were blocking his way, and he had no choice but to stop.

"The President is waiting for me," he said. I am Volmen.

"We know" replied one of the two. Come, come on, accompany you.

They turned, leaving a gap between them, and Volmen, without saying a word, stepped in the middle, and thus they crossed the threshold.

The room was different from the ship that Kronos occupied

Circular and with a shiny floor, an equivalent to the wax that was used in the twentieth century for such a task, but with a huge advantage over that; that never faded.

And the table in the center.

Large, circulate too, and the President, with the Members of the Council.

Six, in all.

One for each of the Continents, counting the one that millennia ago was formed at the South Pole of the Planet.

Volmen was impressed by those silent presences even more so by the brilliant and enigmatic gaze of the President, whose cadaverous face, with sunken sockets, and no less sunken cheekbones, seemed to have the same shine as the ground on which he was treading. instant.

"You are Volmen, who lives with Frida, right?

He leaned a little closer, his own fixed on the President's.

"Why do you ask if you already know? "answered.

"Just answer and nothing else.

Did not answer.

"You are Volmen, right?

"I am Volmen.

"And do you live with Frida?

"I live with Frida" he repeated.
"Sit down.
Steeling himself, Volmen did so in the only chair available, realizing that he was going to be judged by the Six, for something he had no idea of, and trembled.
But he was wrong.

CHAPTER V

And he waited with his eyes fixed on the President, noting how the eyes of the rest examined him in silence, which was still much more sinister than any threat.

"You are a friend of Kelf.

It was not a question, but a statement, and Volmen answered with the same words that he had already answered to Frida minutes before:

"It was," he replied coldly.

The enigmatic face before him did not change expression.

"Explain that, will you?

"He wanted to destroy Kronos, and also every Being on the Planet. To all the Robots-Beings.

"Is it a motive?

"For me, enough.

A silence followed, which grew thick until the President deigned to break it with a piped voice:

"What do you know about him?

"From Kelf?

"Yes.

"Any. Apparently, he has managed to escape from the Big City.

"No one can escape the power of Kronos, or mine.

"I know. But you are mortal.

"What do you mean?

"That you may have mistakes ... but no, Kronos.

Another silence, now shorter than the last.

"Someone is helping you, Volmen.

He shuddered at that statement said in the same way, in the same tone, and without that hermetic face expressing anything.

"Could be. Kelf has friends in the Big City. We all have them.

"I know too. You're one of them.

For the second time, Volmen shuddered.

"Are you trying to accuse me of having done it?

"Not yet, but there is something I want to find out.

"And it is.:.?

"Last night. You weren't with Frida. One of the Robots-Guardians saw you in the street, when the sun was rising. Where did you go?

"I went out to see ..., to ..." he hesitated a little, and added, knowing that he had to speak, to say something ": I tried to see Alvia.

"Why?

"Is beautiful.

"And Frida?

"It is too. I was asleep and completely alone when I arrived. So, Kelf was my friend, and the visit, unscheduled, only has a small penalty, and you know it, President. I returned, and when I went out, I heard the alarm. So I hid, knowing what was going to happen, they could mistake me for someone, and no one likes to die without guilt. The day was dawning when I left my hiding place, since things seemed calmer, and I went home.

That had every sign of being true, and the President asked a new question:

"What did Frida say to you when you arrived? What questions did he ask you?

Volmen held his breath.

At last, he had understood.

Perhaps the President, warned by one of the Robots-Guardians, had seen Frida outside the house, as they saw him, even though he could not realize the fact.

He replied:

"He was not in the house.

"Do not...?

Silence.

Terrifying, even though it didn't last many seconds,

"Answer, Volmen; Where did frida go?

"When she came back, late in the day, she said she had gone shopping, but I didn't believe her.

"So according to you, he was out all night.

"Yes.

"With whom?

Volmen waited for the question, and didn't blink.

"Maybe with Kelf" he coldly replied.

"How do you know?

"She did not give me children. He does not feel love for me.

"Kronos assigned it to you.

"I know, and I followed that order, but she didn't.

"Why?

"For the children. He did not give them to me nor will he ever give them to me,

"Did Frida tell you?

"There are things that do not need to be said.

The President took several seconds to answer, while the rest of the Council Members were silent, but taking notes.

"Leave now

He was surprised at the unexpected command, but got to his feet.

"To my house?

"Do not. Alvia is with Kronos. Go and help her, and watch her. Alvia is precious to Kronos and to the Council.

"And Frida?

"Don't do anything if you see her, if you see her, do you understand? But if so, and he asks, you can tell him about this interview, but decorate it in your own way. And now go, Volmen. And watch out for Alvia. You answer me with ...

"I know what I'm exposing myself to," he replied, turning around to stand between the two Robots-Guardians who were waiting for him.

He went out, before the silence of the grave.

When they were alone, the President looked at them, one by one, then fixed his eyes on Siegel.

"What news is there from your Continent? "I ask.

Short, stocky, he looked like an intelligent animal, not just any other thing.

"We couldn't find whoever made that call.

"How is that?

Siegel could have replied that for the same reason that Kronos could not find Kelf's whereabouts, but he was careful not to mention it, and what he replied was:

"He escaped.

"What is it ...?

"Simply that he escaped. When my Guardians found the place where it should be, that thing was no longer there.

"How do you explain that?

Without losing his usual calm, Siegel replied:

"He just went the way he came.

"Yes...? And where did it go? Kronos will want to know

"To the stars. It came from there, President.

"From the stars ...? That's crazy! A thing of the stars, traveling through space towards us just to warn Kelf not to ... to give up. You're making fun of me, Siegel.

"I knew that would be your reaction…, but I bring you the proof that I am telling the truth. Samples of the place where the ship it was carrying landed, and how everything around it was left when it took off.

"Give them to me!

And she reached out her gnarly hand towards him, equipped with long, sharp nails.

The same as if it were those of a claw. And Siegel handed them over.

CHAPTER VI

She couldn't sleep, she couldn't sit still, nothing could be born except waiting for Volmen.
He feared that arrival.
And as she meditated in that way, Frida thought of Kelf, wondering, in her mind, if he was still where she left him, if he would fulfill the promise he made to wait for her.
It was true that he could leave the house right then and there, but no less true that there were Guardian-Robots nearby.
It would be enough for one of them to see her leave for her to warn the Great House, and Kronos would send her to follow or stop, and both were bad for Kelf as well as for herself.
There they would make her speak.
He would have to, even if he didn't want to.
He thought of Alvia.
Still in the Great House, or with Volmen?
They could be together, of course, on the ship from which Kronos directed the destinies of the Great City and the Planet.
The window and the bed, the bed and the window, until finally, completely surrendered, Frida fell asleep.
When he woke up, it was twelve o'clock on the new day.
Volmcn had not returned.
He went to the window.
The street, apparently, was the same as every day, but there were Robot-Guardians who patrolled it from one place to another.
Frida moved away from there.
The intense search for Kelf continued, it was as if Kronos had the complete assurance that he had not left the city.
Frida remembered what was scheduled for that day, but Volmen was not by her side to help her complete it.
Do it all alone?
The Fountain, the walk, the trees, love next to the whispering waters of a stream.
It was ridiculous!
The food was prepared, but he could barely get through a bite, and when he had finished, once more, he went to the window.
The Robots-Guardians were gone.
Smiled.
Wait for the night.

Hours of impatience, in the course of which Volmen could introduce himself, and he didn't want to in any way.

Go out on the street?

Even if he didn't want to, he had to.

The present day, what was left of it, was for her alone, for apparently Kronos had forgotten to rule her destiny, if only for the moment.

Did.

At the door, on the sidewalk, Frida looked around her, and began to walk.

She was satisfied.

Everything seemed calm, calm, as if Kelf had not existed or as if the fact had never been consummated, but it was not like that.

He looked back.

Nothing nor nobody.

The crowd, going arm in arm with the other crowd of the opposite sex, or simply by their side, slowly moving towards the places of recreation, recreation, programmed in advance.

He touched his breasts.

Inside, between the flesh and the material with which she was dressed, rested the cosmic ray gun, capable of pulverizing one of those buildings that she had to her right or to her left.

He turned left as soon as he reached the second turning, and continued walking on the sidewalk, apparently indifferent to everything that was happening around him, although it was not like that, far from it.

He saw them, a few minutes later.

Two Robots-Guardians, one in each door frame that gave access to the interior of the house that Kelf inhabited, in the company of Alvia.

Frida made a move to step back, thinking that she must have already foreseen it, but they too would make her discover.

He approached, went to ask a question, but the Robot was ahead of his wishes.

"You are Frida, right?

"I'm the one you say" she replied, trying not to lose her calm.

"What do you want?

See Alvia.

"Why?

The Robot's metallic eyes were fixed on hers, and Frida wondered if he was already transmitting his answer, and even his talking image, to the Great House.

"It's my friend" he replied. The President knows.

"Is not sufficient.

"Why?

"I am not programmed to answer questions, but to ask them. Go away, Frida.

The girl bit her lip.

Where can I see it?

"To who?

"To Alvia.

"In the Big House, but you will not be able to pass. Go home, Frida, and rest.

He turned, turning his back, and continued walking, now in reverse. In one of the main streets he went to see a public show, with the spirit willing to make the best of the hours that were left until nightfall, but he could not.

The thought, and especially the memory of Kelf, did not leave her.

She loved Kelf, she had always loved him, but Kronos sent her to live with a Being like Volmen.

The stars, the bright lights that like suns turned the Great City into an ember of light.

Frida started walking.

Moving further and further away from what in the twentieth century was called the urban area of the city, looking for a way out.

She did not want to take a vehicle, knowing that sooner or later the Robot-Driver would call Kronos, saying that they saw her outside the house at that hour,

Launch pads ...

Without knowing it, Frida was thinking about the same thing that Kelf already thought, to, after a few seconds, reach the same conclusion as that one.

The President or Kronos would launch ships in search of them, they would disintegrate them long before they could leave the Galaxy in which the Planet moved. Galaxy I. It was horrible.

Two Guardian-Robots appeared almost in front of her and, with a terrified look as her right hand approached her breasts, she leaped into the dark portal within her grasp, a couple of yards to her right and ahead. her.

He had the strange pistol in his hand when he hit one of the walls and paid attention to his metallic steps on the sidewalk he had just left.

She heard them speak, and her heart, despite being armed, sank.

But they passed by.

Frida sighed, satisfied, put the weapon away, left the portal and continued walking.

CHAPTER VII

"Kelf ..., Kelf ... Are you there, Kelf ...?
He took a couple more steps under the stalactite dome and whispered:
"Come on, Kelf ... are you there ...?
Then she saw him, appearing before her eyes, and coming from one of the corners of the cavern, not smiling, but examining her from head to toe, exactly as if she had never seen her before.
"You have taken a long time, Frida. About twenty hours he "looked at his watch." Eleven o'clock "he said", day or night?
"It is night, Kelf. Engrave it in your memory, in case one day I can't come. Oh, Kelf ...!
And with a slight cry, she ran into his arms.
After kissing her, still in his arms, he whispered:
"Come, Kelf, we will have dinner together. I haven't done it yet.
He seized her around the waist, and they approached the small cave where they had spent the night before.
"Are you going to stay?
"Yes.
"That's dangerous.
"I know.
"And even so...?
"Still, I'm going to do it.
But it was not until halfway through that, when Frida began to speak seriously.
"I was at your house" he began.
He looked into his eyes.
Kelf's grays were impassive.
"Y...?
"I couldn't see Alvia.
Kelf waited, seemingly uninterested in what he had to say, but he wasn't, and Frida understood.
"There were Watch Robots-Guardians. I spoke to one of them, Kelf.
He continued to be silent so the young woman continued:
"He told me that he was in the Great House. With Kronos or with the President. That I couldn't find out.
"And Volmen?
Frida made a face of disgust.
"I'm with you, right?
"Is it an answer?

"It is, Kelf. I love you; I always loved you, and now I don't think you can doubt it,
But there was something more important than that, and they both knew it.
It was Kelf himself who put his finger on the sore, as they say, by asking:
"How long am I going to be here, Frida?
He looked into his eyes.
"Going out meant death for you.
"Staying here, at least for me, has the same meaning.
"Explain that to me, will you?
"This is beautiful, if it weren't so sinister, at least in its meaning. You can visit ... with another Being of the opposite sex.
"As in our case?
"Yes, it is, but for a few hours, and not forever, you understand?
"I think so" she looked at him thoughtfully, and continued with a question:
"What are you planning to do, Kelf?
And there was anguish in her voice, which he pretended not to hear.
"Go out.
"Tonight? That's crazy.
"Tonight, no, Frida, because I have you here, but I'll do it as soon as you stop coming.
"I will never do it.
"Volmen will look for you. You will do it now, if you are not already doing it. As soon as he notices your absence, he will notify any of the Robots ...
"And that worries you, Kelf?
"Yes. Not to you?
"No." He paused slightly, and added, "Listen, Kelf, there is a way out. You get it right? Launching ramps. You have one weapon and I have another. We can finish with the Robot-Rocket and ..., and ... I will accompany you to the stars. I want to be with you forever, Kelf.
"They would finish us off before we made it out of Galaxy I.
"We will die together.
"That's not going to ...
Frida interrupted him, almost violently:
"It will be so, it is decided. I can't go back to Volmen's side. I neither can nor want, you understand? "He hesitated a bit, and continued, after a few seconds of silence": I am going to try to check for myself the vigilance that is on the ramps, and return to your side. If all goes well, we'll go out together and ...
"Will you go now?
Frida smiled at him.

"Do not. I will leave at sunrise, and for your peace of mind I will tell you that I will not enter the Big City. From here, the ramps can be reached, without any of the Robot-Guardians seeing me. Come on, finish dinner.

He did not respond, but his agile electronic computer brain was working at peak performance until finally, they had dinner.

Then the question arose on Kelf's mouth:

"You still haven't told me if you saw Volmen, Frida.

She walked over to him, took one of his hands and almost forced him to encircle her waist.

"Is that necessary, Kelf? He asked in a whisper and brushing her right ear with his lips.

"Yes. I think so.

"Okay, I saw Volmen.

"Y...?

"I always keep my promises,

"Nothing more?

"Could there be something else?

"No, maybe not," Kelf replied thoughtfully, "but I'd like to know what happened.

So Frida explained everything to him.

"Nothing more...?

"But, Kelf ... I ...

He was already kissing him without finishing the sentence, so now the embrace between the two lasted a long time, and nevertheless, Frida left him with the dawn exactly as she had promised.

The rock closed behind her and, in front of her, already lit with the clarity of the new day, she saw the path that would lead to that other that closed the passageway and led directly to her house, without taking the detour that she had taken the night before. to go see Kelf, thus avoiding going back there, in case he ran into Volmen.

Then hesitated

Once again, and now in broad daylight, she had to make a wide detour, toward the launch pads, without passing, as she had already told Kelf, through the Great City, where they would be waiting for her. Volmen, between them. Volmen and Alvia.

She kept walking, her right hand at the level of her breasts, for a few minutes.

There were six of them, which appeared before his sight from as many points and, when he saw them, he understood that all was lost.

Even Kelf, her lover of a few hours, was. She raised her hand and pulled down that kind of blouse she was wearing, the fabric ripped and the weapon sprouted in her hand.
Mad with terror, terrified, the aggression started from the.
Shooting.
In front of his eyes there was a blue spark, a tongue of fire, and the Robot-Guardian disappeared from his retinas as the tree directly behind him became a brand that also vanished in a matter of a fifth of a second. Not without Frida noticing the heat wave on her back that almost knocked her to the ground.
The second cosmic ray brushed his hair and he was lost in the mountain, with the boom of thunder, and he squeezed the trigger a second time.
Another of the Robots disappeared from the planet, turned into multicolored sparks, but Frida never saw it because at that precise moment one of the rays struck her.
He didn't notice anything.
It just disappeared.
On the ground, where his feet had been, there was only a slight stain on the grass.

* * *

"Are you watching me, Volmen?
"Me...?
There was a silence, as he stared at her.
Both were in the house of Kelf, after having been subjected, once again, but now in common, to endless questions.
Then they left the Great House, very close together, and after dinner that night, the question arose on her lips.
"You do not answer? Come on, Alvia, what makes you guess this?
She looked around.
"All this," he said, with a strange intonation in his voice. Was it Kronos who ordered it, or did the President just do it?
"I do not understand you.
"Do not...?
"Of course not, Alvia. I spoke with Kronos and with the President. That's true, and we both know it.
"About what?
"Of you. I asked him to let you come with me.
" Y...?
"Now you're here.

"Which means they accepted, right?

"Yes that's how it is.

"I do not like.

Volmen looked at her in surprise

"Why ? "I ask". You always loved me, Alvia.

"Yes," she replied, unperturbed, with terrifying coldness. But not this way.

"There is another? Kronos chooses and nothing else. Now Frida doesn't count. They are looking for her with orders to kill her, to make her disappear from the planet. They know it helped Kelf.

"And let them know, you have taken care of it, right?

"Yes that's how it is. What I feel is not knowing where he is.

"Would you go find him?

"Of course.

"Only?

"Yes.

Alvia let a few seconds of silence elapse, and then, suddenly, she went back to what she had said before.

"We were talking about Kronos.

"I know. You said ...

-That I didn't like this.

"Why?

"Because my feelings don't count. Neither mine nor the others. Only the opposite sex. Yours, Volmen. All you have to do is ask, wish, and Kronos will grant it.

"And you do not like it?

"Do not.

"Not with me?

"Not even with you, Volmen.

He narrowed his eyes.

"You're talking like Kelf, Alvia. It is so, even if you don't realize it.

Alvia glared at him.

"I'm not thinking like him, far from it," he declared. It is a feeling. An idea.

"There are no ideas, Alvia.

"That's what Kronos says, but thinking ... Well, it doesn't fade. Nor the right to have ideas either.

"They were erased when Kronos entered the Power of the Planet.

Alvia did not want to argue and, seeing that she was silent, Volmen rose, walked around the table and approached.

His big hands went to her shoulders, and Alvia raised her head to look at him.

She was leaning on her lips ... and she wanted him as she never wanted anything, but she instinctively pulled away from him when he tried to kiss her.
Volmen, without letting go, looked at her carefully.
"What is the matter with you, Alvia? "I ask.
"Kelf.
Volmen released her and took a few steps back. Then he cursed under his breath.
"What about Kelf?
"Still lives.
"That doesn't count for Kronos.
"But yes for me" he left the place where he sat and openly confronted him by adding "If you want, Volmen, you can tell the President. Kill Kelf, and you will have me, but not before.
"I'm not going to tell you any of that. Neither Kronos nor ...
I was no longer listening to him.
Turning around, Alvia walked away from him, heading for the door that led to the bedroom.
Volmen didn't move, just looked at her, until suddenly he called out to her.

CHAPTER VIII

The four of them looked at each other.
The silence was impressive, until one of them broke it with a question:
"Did you see the rock?
"We saw it.
And Kelf may be behind.
"Kelf is behind" affirmed the fourth. But you have to be careful. Kronos has prepared something for him, far worse than death.
"You know?
"Do not. Just the order. It has to be alive, or it will destroy us.
They no longer spoke.
The four Robots-Guardians began to separate from each other, tracing a mortal semicircle, in the center of which was the huge rock that closed the entrance to the bowels of the Planet.
Then they stopped.
The distance was convenient.
Now or never.
The Robot-Guardian-Chief thought so, but didn't say so.
He simply raised his armed hand and the lightning went off.
The rock made a click, a spark, and cracked all the way down the length and breadth, but did not give way.
"You have to be careful now" he said to the others who, like statues, completely immobile, contemplated the scene.
He adjusted the gun and raised it.
On the other side of the rock, in the center of the cavern, Kelf leaped sideways, carrying his, and clung to one of the walls, eyes fixed on the other side, toward the entrance, which seemed to be locked up. and singing.
The ground shook.
Above his head, the stalactites cracked ominously.
Another volley of that kind, and the roof would collapse, burying him.
He thought of Frida.
What had become of Frida?
Did they see her get out of there?
It was the safest thing to do, as well as that they had followed her to the entrance of the cavern, but not long enough to get inside.
The rest, the rest, was terrifyingly simple.
While, oblivious to what was happening outside, they loved and embraced each other, Death had been stalking them.

Alvia and Volmen in the Great House.

Frida had told him, and Volmen ...

Well, he was able to put the President in the background, rightly suspecting that she was with him, that she had to be followed, that there was ...

Something like distant thunder erupted in front of him, he saw the light, almost blinding him, and the entrance rock pulverized, exposing the wide gap.

And the clarity of the sun, tarnished by dust and debris that began to fall from the ceiling.

Clinging to the walls, perspiring, breathing in the nauseating smell of melted stone, Kelf staggered a few steps toward the gap that he was now beginning to see with perfect clarity.

With more clarity with each passing second, and as the dust was diminishing, while behind him, as he was leaving it behind, the ceiling began to collapse, with the noise of hell.

Outside, very close to the entrance, the four Guardian-Robots were adjusting their weapons to NOT KILL.

Inside, his back pressed against the rough edges of the rock, Kelf slid toward the exit.

He knew he had to hurry, or he would never catch up with her.

"Kelf ...

I do not answer.

Behind him, the thunder of the collapse increased in intensity.

The entire mountain was swaying.

"Kelf ... Get out of there, Kelf ... or you will die. Kronos wants to see you. He wants you to introduce yourself to the Council. The President wants it too.

He thought of Frida.

What had they done with Frida?

And he did not answer.

He kept on advancing, the short, thick barrel of the gun pointed straight ahead and his finger taut on the self-timer.

How many charges did he have left?

He didn't know or care, at the time.

The ground parted almost at his feet, and he staggered further, grasping the ledges of the rock wall with the fingers and nails of his left hand.

The movement of the ground stabilized.

It was a few seconds, maybe less, and maybe it would open completely, taking it with it to the depths of the planet.

"Kelf ...

The noise almost deafened him, so he did not hear that new call.

A few yards away from his body, something fell from the ceiling, and the cloud of dust enveloped him, causing him to cough.

Then he jumped, but he did not land on his feet on the other side of the doorway, but rolled on himself, while the rays they now sent at him, paralyzing, he suspected, made light clicks around him.

He opened fire.

Once, twice, three and even four times, and he saw them burn in an infernal blaze, and disappear from his sight, as perhaps Frida disappeared.

He stood up, taking a deep breath.

Behind him, always behind him, with a horrible crash, the ceiling of the cavern collapsed, and the seismic movement it produced threw him first on his face, and then rolling several yards away.

Broken, panting, sweaty, bruised and scratched, Kelf rose to his feet, still holding the weapon.

After the earthquake after the thunder of the collapse, the silence was impressive.

Kelf looked back.

More than half a mountain had sunk into the interior of the Planet, and before his eyes there was only a desolate panorama of broken rocks, shattered trees and crevices, hideous cracks in the earth and in the rock.

He averted his eyes and looked around.

Kelf called Frida.

Once, twice, several more times, and then he spent more than three hours looking for her, until he convinced himself that he would not see her anymore.

Then he started walking.

The so-called modern laboratory of the late twentieth century, in its distant time.

The lethal gas, discovered by chance, the explosions from the glass tube in his hands ...

He continued walking towards the entrance that gave access to the tunnel that should lead him to Frida's house.

Volmen would be there, waiting for her, but she would never come.

Frida had canceled, once and for all, all her appointments.

The gas ... the explosion, and later, the awakening.

The Central Hospital of the missing Washington, federal capital of the United States of America.

The bed and its eyes ...

His eyes; he had lost his sight.

The bandages around his head and the mutation.

There was no hope, but the mutation occurred within him, without human means being used to do so, and his eyes regained clarity, sight.

The lethal gas, the lost formula ..., and its secret ...

Then the Washington Research Center, and everything else.

For generations, his dead cells were flushed out of his body by living ones, and his biochemical makeup was continually renewed ... as in an age-old nuclear chain reaction.

That was his body, a chain reaction of the millions of cells that made it up, producing a life that could last infinitely ... if Kronos didn't decide otherwise, and apparently it had already decided.

The passageway, the front door.

It took Kelf hours to get to Volmen's house, but now his visit was of a different kind. I could no longer see Frida there but I could see Volmen.

Even if he didn't want to, he would tell her what the Council thought.

Everything he was interested in knowing, including the number of Guardian-Robots on the ramps, and if he could ... the goal was the stars.

Maybe there was an escape route there.

The door, closing its way.

In other words, the hatch above your head.

Kelf pushed her up, and listened without dropping the weapon.

How many charges do you have left ...?

He did not even finish asking the question, the silence inside the house was absolute, so he finished lifting it, and entered the room.

He remembered Frida.

He remembered her as he searched the house.

Volmen was not there.

In his, loving Alvia?

It was possible, if the order had come from Kronos or the President.

The street.

He clung to the walls and walked, trying to stay in the shadows, with his back pressed against the facades of the houses, in the Great City that now, due to its silence, resembled the City of the Dead.

The door.

Kelf hesitated.

All around him, silence.

They were still looking for him.

That was all; Kronos wanted the streets completely clear of pedestrians and road traffic.

Only the Robots-Guardians would be allowed to pass, on foot or in rocket vehicles.

He rummaged in his pockets.

The key; I still had it.

He opened, closed in the same way, without producing a single sound, and entered, the corridor forward to the so-called dining room, where the chairs and tables appeared from the floor, pressing a simple button, from one of the panels on the wall.

None of this was in sight, so he suspected that both Alvia and Volmen were conspicuous by their absence.

He crossed the room and into the bedroom.

There he waited until he heard them enter.

Kelf walked to the door and listened.

Half an hour ... one?

Perhaps it was much less when he moved away from there to go to stand at the opposite end of the bedroom.

* * *

"Alvia.

With her hand brushing the door, she turned to look at him. "Yes.

It was not coming.

Volmen thought so, but didn't say so.

"That phone call ..." he began.

He saw her smile.

He was humanizing himself, as he believed.

"You did it. And you lied to Kronos.

"Everyone lies to Kronos ... but he doesn't know it. It is the only thing you cannot know. On the other hand, you gave me the idea.

"I know. But it was just that, a possibility.

"You proved to know him well ... or you read his mind.

"I don't read anything in mind, Volmen, but, as you say, I know Kelf, I knew he was up to something, and I told you. The rest ... was your doing. Now, if I was wrong ... He laughed.

"The same would have happened. Kronos would have acted the same way. The operator and that call from the other continent were enough to destroy Kelf, even if it was a lie. Do you understand

"Yes, I think so" he paused, which Volmen did not interrupt, and added, after a few seconds of silence: "It came from the stars, as you say, right?" How ... how ...?

Volmen took a step forward, and she took another toward him.

He laughed once more when they faced each other, almost touching.

"I used one of the ramp ships. I destroyed the rocket-robot and ...

"Volmen!

"There is no danger, Alvia. The trip only takes minutes ... long distance, and the warning to Kelf. I wished someone would pick up the call, in case you were wrong in your suspicions, but they were not, and Kelf, despite everything, acted as you expected. Then ... Well, after the call, I came back. Matter of minutes, Alvia.
He moved closer, which seemed completely impossible.
And they didn't see me. Neither when leaving nor when returning. I was able to do it from here. Ask for the continent and, through it, Kelf's house in the Big City, but the operator would have noticed. Now we are both.
She said nothing, but took a step back, pulling away a little.
"Alvia.
"Yes?
"I'm going to stay. You get it right?
Shook his head.
"Kelf is still there, as I told you.
He stepped back a bit; to the door.
Volmen didn't move, he just stared at her.
"Kronos said ...
"You already explained that to me before, and the answer is the same.
"Kelf ...?
"That's how it is. He doesn't count, but he lives on. He and Frida.
"Kronos doesn't care.
She was opening the door when she cocked her head to look at him.
"We talked about this earlier, Volmen.
He finished opening it and Volmen stood there in the center of the room, his eyes fixed on his back.
He also saw how he closed it, after having crossed the threshold.

* * *

Alvia was opening the door.
He hated Alvia; He had always hated her, and not because of herself, but because of Kronos.
Then came the children, and he hated her even more; almost with an irrational hatred, typical of a filthy beast
How she hated him.
Kelf was sure of that.
It was closing behind her, and she blinked a little when she turned on the light.
"Your!
It was a whisper, very slight, but nevertheless he heard with perfect clarity.

He was pointing it at her, and she was looking at him with wide eyes.
"Since ...-, since when have you been here, Kelf ...?
A new whisper, but clear, clear as the glass tube that had exploded millennia
ago in his hands, causing his blindness.
“It's been a long time, although I certainly don't 'know. Come on, Alvia, go
ahead, and sit down. There on the bed. It is a good place for you; the best.
"Kelf ...
"Sit down.
"Kelf ...
"Yes...?
"What ... what are you going to do with me?
“I could finish at once, but I don't want to. I don't want it, despite everything,
do you understand? But I can change my mind. That is up to you to decide.
"What should I do? Do you know about the call ...?
Kelf responded, reversing the order of the questions, by giving the answer:
“I have heard it. Regarding the other ... sit down.
She did not respond for the moment, she approached him, passed him,
brushing against him, also brushing the barrel of the weapon, which kept
pointing her between her breasts, and sat where Kelf indicated.
Thinking about whether Kelf would know that Volmen was in the adjoining
room, in which he served as the dining room, and he said yes, since he
claimed he knew about the call from the mainland; I had heard it.
But what he repeated was:
"What are you going to do with me?
"Talk.
"Only that?
"Yes.
Alvia looked around her.
“They are looking for you, Kelf. Kronos is looking for you all over the
planet.
“That means they think I managed to escape from the Big City.
“That doesn't mean anything, and you know it.
It was a truth; more than that, a great truth.
"I know" he replied, "What are you going to do with me? You know it. You
were in the Great House, with Kronos and Volmen.
“I love Volmen.
"I know" he smiled. I recently heard you say that I would not have you until
I had been killed. If he does, Alvia, Kronos and the President will finish off
you two.
"I know too.

"It was a change of conversation and Kelf did not want it, so he continued as in the beginning.

"Speak, Alvia" he said. I am listening to you. What do the Great House think?

"I do not know. And now you can finish me, Kelf I will not blink or tremble at you. What are you waiting for?

"One more question.

"Yes...?

"The Robot-Guardians of the ramps, Alvia.

She looked at him with wide eyes.

"You are mad, Kelf, if you think you are going to leave the Planet like that!

"I will try ..., and perhaps I will decide to take you with me.

"Kronos would not allow it.

"But I do ... and, he is very far ... despite having him so close. At least for you.

He was thinking of Volmen, who was not coming in, who was there, a few yards from them, and who also carried a weapon.

Exact replica of the one Kelf held in his hand.

"You will not do it.

"Why?

"Because I would kill you, Kelf, even if it was near the stars. You have always hated me because I never wanted to give you a child and because Kronos sent me to you, when you wanted Frida.

Get up, Alvia.

"That...?

"That you stand up ..., and walk towards the door

"For what?

"I want to see Volmen. I know it's there since it came in with you. Kronos sent him, but not for what you think.

"What do you mean?

"Kronos is not yet sure of you, of your participation in my attempt to destroy him, and he is watching you. Nobody better than Volmen to do it. There are no feelings, they are forbidden on the Planet, Alvia, but not when it suits Kronos. That's the truth.

"You cannot affirm that.

"May 1. I'm the only one who can, and you know it too.

Alvia got up, leaving the edge of the bed, and turned toward the door, beginning to walk.

CHAPTER IX

He only took two or three steps, stopped, and faced him:
"What do you want from Volmen, Kelf? Kill him?
"I'm going to tell you about Frida. How Kronos broke up with her. Come on, walk.
Alvia turned the other way, took another step, and the door swung open to frame Volmen in the doorway.
She put her hands to her breasts, stepped aside, and they both squeezed the triggers at the same time, and the two cosmic rays found their destination.
Volmen disappeared with a flash of light, the wall behind him after literally drilling the so-called dining room, the door that gave access to the street and there he lost against the wall of the house on the opposite sidewalk, not without leaving a huge gap, mute witness of its passage.
For his part, Kelf received him full chest, turned around completely, and fell to the ground with his arms and legs crossed, like a disjointed doll.
Wide-eyed, looking at her, seeing her clearly, but unable to move or utter a word.
Aware of what was happening around him, but completely paralyzed.
He saw her lean over him, smiling, lean more and more to his lips, kiss him, take the gun from his hand and move closer to the wall panel.
He unfolded it without losing his smile, he picked up the automatic micro-telephone, brought it to his mouth and said:
"Kelf is here with me. Come find him.
She turned to look at him, after closing the panel, and approached.
"I know you are hearing me, even if you can't see me, Kelf, do you understand? And this is your end. I ... I'm going to join the Council. I will take your place at the table and you ... you will disappear, ..
They were knocking on the door.
He stepped away from her and opened it.
Kelf's eyes followed her even in her slightest movements, as she faced the two Guardian-Robots who came to take him away,
She was beautiful, very beautiful, but he hated her.
He had always hated her.
And he was still smiling when they came to take him away.
But he did not accompany him to the Great House.
It remained there, in which they had shared for a couple of years or three, Kelf did not know for sure because time did not count for him with the beautiful, slanted eyes fixed on the gap that opened the cosmic ray that he launched on Volmen .

Maybe she was thinking about him, maybe she was remembering the past, his caresses and kisses; Or maybe it was simply that, after what happened, and seeing how they took him away, he did not know how to react.
Or maybe he was thinking of Volmen, whom he would never see again.
Kelf didn't know.
He was on the way to the Great House when he lost consciousness.

* * *

They had not tied him up.
That was the first sensation he experienced when he regained it, and he looked around.
They were all sitting around the table, exactly the same as him.
But not in the same chair that he occupied other times, not in that of the Damned.
In front of his own, the President's eyes, and the impressive silence.
He took a deep breath, and waited.
It wasn't much.
The silence was broken by the President himself with a question:
"Are you willing, Kelf?
He knew what it all meant, so he calmly replied:
"Yes.
He turned his head, and then he saw them.
A double row of Robot-Guardians stood along the walls, weapons in hand.
For generations, Kelf had felt important, but never like this time.
Kronos and the Grand Council were afraid.
They were afraid of him; in other words, they weren't sure what he could do against them, despite seeing him there, completely defenseless.
He looked at the President.
The sunken sockets, fixed in his eyes, sparkled like diamonds.
"Come in Alvia.
He did not know who he was giving the order to, nor did he turn his head to look.
Quite simply, Kelf continued to wait, aware of what his destiny would be from now on, but he was wrong all along the line.
She heard a faint hum, to her left, and guessed that the wall was opening to one side to let her pass, but she didn't look.
He remained motionless, impassive.
And it continued in the same way when Alvia entered the range of his eyes, and approached the table.

She stopped, her hands behind her back, cold and impassive, distant, in silence, waiting for the next question that was not long in coming.
"Did you know that Kelf was going to destroy Kronos?
"Do not. He never told me
"Why?
"Kelf hated me.
"Explain that.
"He has feelings. He also has ideas and that is forbidden on the planet. And those feelings went to Frida, who lived with Volmen.
"What else?
"He never wanted children, and Kronos ordered that we have them.
"You are telling the truth?
"Yes
There was a slight silence, which the President, in his role as Interrogator, broke:
"Did you see how he killed Volmen?
"Yes. Kelf did it in front of my eyes.
Another new pause, which the President ended with one more question, but this one addressed to Kelf:
"What do you have to add to what Alvia said, Kelf?
"Any.
Alvia looked at him in surprise.
Undoubtedly, he was not expecting that answer, spoken in a cold and impersonal tone, as if indeed he did not care about the trial that was being held against him before the Members of the Council, to whom he belonged until he had the idea of destroying Kronos.
"You can go home, Alvia" replied the President. And wait there. Kronos will alert you. Did not answer.
Silently, he turned and walked over to the panel. The buzzing repeated, but Kelf didn't even look at it.
Exactly like minutes before, his eyes were fixed on the President, who was looking at him again, while the other Members remained speechless, but without ceasing to observe him:
"Why did you want to destroy Kronos?
"He is ending the Robots-Beings. One way or another it does.
"What do you mean?
Kelf let a few seconds of silence elapse before answering, when he finally did, his voice rose a bit in pitch:
"It is turning us into Robots, taking away our Being. You, President, all those and me. And those of the opposite sex.
"Those are ideas, Kelf.

"I have them, and it can't be helped. You can't help it, and you know it. Kronos, too.

"He is the only one who can have them. Kronos is Thinking.

"I know. But I gave him my ideas, my power, now he can't ask me not to have them. You, and a few others like you, President, helped me with the task and then he created the machines. To the Robot-Beings, who by strange paradox, believe in the Planet and at the same time destroy it.

"I do not understand that.

"Do not...? Well, if so, President, go to one of the disintegrators yourself and finish with yourself. It is a solution. Kronos orders and the others obey. That was the idea, but up to a point. We cannot think, we cannot have ideas, and we are controlled down to the smallest details. Even in love. Therefore, Kronos must be destroyed.

There was a murmur, which was cut off as quickly as it had started when the President raised one of his hands, staring at him with strange fixation.

"You are crazy, Kelf! "Was what he said, after a few seconds of silence.

Kelf rose to his feet, dominating them with his stature with the Power that seemed to emanate from his titan figure.

"I have ideas, President" he stated coldly. Ideas that will change the Planet.

"Kronos doesn't want it, Kelf. And that's all.

"Everything...?

"You cannot have ideas. Those are from Kronos. Therefore, you are a danger, which must disappear. He became a Thinker, and now he does it for everyone. They are the rules. He also gave you Alvia, and you turned her down. You saw his statement, Kelf, and that, in itself, is the end. The sentence is... death, but you are not going to die.

"Do not...?

There was strangeness in his voice, but neither of them noticed.

"Do not. Kronos gives you something more ... more spectacular. Turn your back.

"What you have to do will be straight ahead.

There was a hesitation, a slight doubt, which the President cut off:

"Nothing is going to happen to you, Kelf. They are orders from Kronos, and he doesn't lie. We just want you to see one thing for yourself.

Just then, Siegel raised his hand, and the President's ghastly face turned to him.

"Do you want to ask a question, Siegel? He inquired.

"Just one.

"Make it.

He looked at Kelf.

"There was a call from the Continent, Kelf" he said. The operator said someone told you not to do something. Was it the destruction of Kronos? "Yes.

"Who was your communicator?

"I do not know.

Siegel thought quickly, perhaps realizing that it was not just one question he was asking, but several more, and he launched another:

"You mean you don't know the identity of the thing that came from the stars to communicate with you?

"From the stars ...? "He laughed, and added when the excess of hilarity let him do it": No one came from the stars to warn me. That is another lie for me. of Kronos and the Great Council.

"That's it, President," Siegel replied.

But he did it when he was already standing with his gnarled hands on the table, staring at him.

"The trial is over, Kelf" he said. And now turn your back to the table. I must show you something.

He no longer doubted.

It did so slowly, while a slight buzzing sounded again, but different from the one that preceded Alvia's entrance into the Great Council Room.

In front of him, less than half a yard away, the ground began to lift and a metal table appeared.

A table and a glass with a colorless liquid inside.

"Drink that, Kelf.

The buzzing had stopped, and the table was still.

"Is it Death? "I ask.

"It's the Journey, Kelf. Kronos is not going to kill you.

What does that trip mean?

"Drink and you will know.

He shrugged, held out his hand; he took the glass or its equivalent, and raised it to his lips.

Kelf drank.

He noticed neither smell nor taste, and made a move to turn towards the table, but could not complete the turn because before his mind clouded, and he fell rolling to the floor.

He woke up much later, hours, days, months, or years later.

Kelf had lost track of time-space.

He looked around, experiencing the sensation that he was floating in emptiness and that his body was lying on something soft.

He looked and saw the straps.

A bunk.

AND UNDERSTOOD!

Kronos hadn't lied.

He was traveling, perhaps to the stars, and he wondered why.

His mind, completely lucid, asked question after question, while his hands, working independently with his brain, went to the straps.

He stood up.

He wore magnetic soles, which kept him glued to the floor of the circular cabin.

Circular and huge.

The journey would be long.

He understood it when he saw the control panel, where the lights went on and off, the TV screen, and especially the controls.

He knew how to handle them.

Kelf advanced to the panels.

He opened one, crossed the ship to the other side, and repeated the operation with the second.

Bright stars and blackness of hell.

The Cosmos on both sides, and the impressive silence of space that also seemed to have taken over the spaceship inside which he was at that moment.

Even when?

CHAPTER X

Kelf tried to fix them on his retinas, comparing them to the thousands and thousands he had seen on previous trips, and was unsuccessful.
Stars and constellations, which seemed to ride through space, fast backwards, always backwards.
He walked away from there.
The sensation of weightlessness did not exist inside the starship.
The lights continued to flicker in front of his eyes, coming from the dashboard, and the television screen remained completely blank.
Pushing one of the buttons, trying to get in touch ... with whom?
With nobody.
There would be no contact.
However, he could turn the ship around and bring it back to the Planet.
But no, it wouldn't be possible either; Kronos and the President would have planned everything, so that he would not return, or, if not, he would have already died.
Like Frida.
FRIDA!
He had completely forgotten her.
Slowly now, Kelf approached the control panel, and his fingers, independent of the dictates of his brain, fiddled with the buttons, while his avid eyes took in everything in front of him.
Studying the control of the spaceship down to its smallest details, but without being able to remove from his mind the question that haunted him.
Where were they sending him? What was its orbit?
Through the Cosmos, without Beyond?
I did not know, I did not know it.
Back, back ...
He knew he couldn't, for the reasons given above, and yet after a few long seconds of hesitation, Kelf seized one of the controls and pulled towards himself, trying to divert the intersideral ship from its path.
It did not succeed.
Conversely, trying to get him to make a left turn, looking at the electronic dials, and now he did, but it was very little.
Three degrees no more, but on her own, once she released the control, she straightened her course and continued walking in the void.
At that precise moment, the red indicator on the screen in front of him lit up and, helplessly, Kelf realized that it was going to light up, and he held his breath.
It was like this.

In a confused way at first, and with perfect clarity later, he saw before him the cadaverous face of the President.

Beside him, the always beautiful Alvia, who was smiling at him.

"Hello, Kelf, I suppose you are enjoying the trip. As I promised you in front of the Great Council, you have not died, but you set out on your way. And you will not return to the Planet. Do not try, as before, because you will fail.

Kelf didn't reply.

His eyes seemed to look only at Alvia, perhaps because he knew she saw him too, perhaps thousands of miles away.

"Do you hear me, Kelf?

Now he did answer:

"Perfectly.

"Don't try it because ...

"I already heard it.

"Any clarification?

"Some. I would like to know...

"I know what you want to know, Kelf" interrupted the President, "and I'm going to tell you. Listen carefully, that this is the first and last contact with you, so there will be no opportunity to repeat it. Are you ready?

"I am.

"There is no orbit in the trip, Kelf. No, so it can last for millions of years, until the ship you are traveling in disintegrates because it is old or is going to collide with an asteroid or with any of the planets that you may encounter on your way "he paused and asked": Together on your left hand there is a yellow button, Kelf, do you see it?

"Yes.

"It will light up four times as you walk through space. Only four, with intervals of three thousand light years each. Only then can you steer the ship as you please, and for twenty-four hours. Long enough for you to find a planet to rest on… to stay, if you wish. If you do not like it, it will be enough for you to return before those twenty-four hours because, if you do not, you will have to stay once and for all, since the ship will take flight completely alone. And keep one thing in mind, whether you are inside or not, you will never reach the Planet because, after the specified time period, the automatic pilot, which can only be disconnected from here, will keep it on the course that now go on. Anything else, Kelf?

"Only one thing," he answered quickly, and with a calm so cold that thousands of miles away, he made Alvia open her eyes, in unusual amazement.

"I hear you.

"What will happen when yellow shines for the last time?

"You will choose another planet, another star, but it will be your last chance.
"And if I do not do it?
"You will travel eternally, Kelf, for millions of years, or until you end your life yourself, Kelf crashing the ship against any obstacle. Don't forget that you can do it. Three degrees to the left for four minutes is more than enough.
A few seconds of silence followed.
On the screen, Alvia kept her eyes fixed on him, without a single blink.
Located to the right of the President, neither his eyes, nor his face, always beautiful, perfect, let his emotions shine through, if he actually had any at that moment.
Kelf himself broke it, with a question:
"How long have I been here, unconscious?
"Three days, Kelf. Something insignificant, if we did not take into account that you are moving away from Kronos at a speed three times faster than light.
He shuddered, unable to help it.
It was ... as if the Grand Council, and with it Kronos himself, were sending him to the ends of the Universe.
Outside the Universe itself.
"To survive, you will find tablets and supplies on the ship, Kelf. Kronos thinks of everything. This will last you thousands of years ... but you will have to descend from the ship, like it or not, to continue living. Your biochemical makeup didn't take your dietary needs into account, Kelf.
"Yes I know. Anything else I need to know?
"That's all" he cocked his head to look at Alvia, and asked Kelf "Do you want to tell her something?
Kelf shook his.
"No" he replied. Any.
Alvia didn't say a word either, but now she was smiling.
"Wait a minute, Kelf.
"Yes...?
"You can light up this screen at will, do you understand? You will be able to see your own life and what you want. And things on the planet. With that, you won't forget it.
Kelf said nothing.
Alvia's eyes haunted him.
Eyes that smiled, the same as his red mouth, like a bleeding wound.
That I would never see.
Suddenly the screen went black, and Kelf felt infinitely small.
Three days traveling at that speed ...

He shook his head, he did not want to continue thinking, but it was impossible for him to do so, so he turned on the screen.

Pieces almost forgotten or completely forgotten, of his past, began to parade before his eyes.

So over and over again, many more, until The INFINITE appeared in front of him.

Time did not count.

Nor the arms, the kisses and caresses of Frida or Alvia. and that of as many and as many women as they loved him, in those thousands of years of longevity.

Nothing counted for him anymore, not even his own existence.

In the Cosmos, the intersideral ship continued its inexorable march, leaving behind the suns, the stars, new Constellations never seen from the Planet of the Galaxy I.

Again and again the laboratory, the explosion, the inhalation of the lethal gas and the mutation, whose first effects reached their eyes, making them regain new sight when the science of that time had already concluded everything.

The years, Alvia, Kronos, Frida ..., and that call to warn him not to do it, not to move from his house at least until he spoke with his communicator. She should have waited for him.

Volmen, the Great Council, of which he was a part on the Planet, as the Being-Robot that gave life and shape to Kronos.

Kelf slept and ate like an automaton, wondering a thousand times if space wasn't mining his brain.

Or maybe it was Time.

But time did not count in the Universe, or in the Past, Present or Future. There was no Future there.

Only a ship and a Journey as infinite as infinity itself where it had to be found for centuries.

Kelf snapped out of his apathy when, suddenly, the yellow button flickered in front of his eyes, then froze.

Switched on.

Hesitating, he approached the controls, and took them, then touching them with his fingertips.

Nothing happened.

Then he tried to deflect the ship to his right and, with a docility that surprised him, was obeyed.

TWENTY FOUR HOURS!

That was how long he had.

At that speed, more than enough to find a planet, perhaps inhabited by other beings, even if they were different from it.
Kelf longed for company, whatever it was.
Kronos knew how to do things well with him.
But he was out of luck.
After a curve that took him six and a half hours, Kelf started the jet engines, and descended to the crust of an asteroid.
Inhospitable, materially covered in limestone rock and cosmic dust, about a thousand square miles.
A kind of island in the Cosmos that traveled at twice the speed of sound, curving towards the sun, which he saw shining like a golden ember through the glasses he was wearing.
On the other side, the shadow.
Invisibility, if it could be called that.
Discouraged, after three more hours of exploration, wearing a space suit and special shoes, he returned to the ship, closed the doors tightly, took a couple of tablets, and stretched out on the bunk, adjusting the straps.
He fell asleep.
When he woke up, he was traveling again, having the sun on his left and the stars of a new constellation on his right.
He turned on the screen.
It would have been much better to finish at once, to finish like Frida or Volmen, and like so many and so many others, before challenging the Power of Kronos, a Power that he himself had created, to be destroyed by that same Power.
Again and in front of his eyes, all his past slipped away, and he saw again the faces of Frida and Volmen, and his, with Alvia.
Wars, catastrophes, and the first Council of the Planet to deal with Kronos. His attempt- at destruction, the telephone voice from the other Continent, and his escape, after getting rid of the Robots-Guardians.
The screen was blank.
Kelf got up and, for a long time, remained with his eyes fixed on the constellations on his right, while on his left the sun that had illuminated him up to that moment began to disappear rapidly in the distance,
Then the blackness of space enveloped everything, like a mortal cloak.
He returned to the bunk and lay down.
Kelf fell asleep, caressed by Frida's loving arms.
But Frida no longer existed.

* * *

Kelf discovered the planet when only half an hour ago the yellow light on the dashboard had come on.

He lit up the screen, as the gauges showed him the celestial body moving almost in front of him, at a distance of fifty thousand miles.

He began to slow the ship, which automatically obeyed.

To his left, somewhat elevated above what we might call the horizon of the spacecraft, the sun that illuminated the planet remained fixed in space.

Exactly like the one that kept alive the beings that populated the planet.

The screen lit up.

Kelf held his breath and looked.

It was still far, far away, but it would soon be within reach.

The lost formula, the secret that will accompany you for millennia ...

He shook his head to keep from thinking.

The distance was closing more slowly now.

The ship's brakes worked perfectly.

Later, after reading the data that the ship's instruments would show him, about the density and gravity of the planet, its atmospheric composition and so many and many other things about it, he would tilt the spacecraft, looking for the right angle to enter its atmosphere. .

He did it over a cloudy area, and the memory of the Planet and Kronos fired in his mind in such a way that, for a few seconds, the rhythmic beating of his heart was altered, thinking that it could be that one.

It was not.

He knew it as soon as he crossed the barrier of clouds, while, in front of his eyes and at fantastic speed across the television screen, rivers, seas, mountains, valleys, grass and lakes glided.

It was not the Planet, but it had an atmosphere and plant life.

The other ... might or might not exist, but at the moment, Kelf didn't care, not a little, not a lot.

At that moment he wanted only one thing, to descend on its surface.

But he did not rush.

Kelf took height, after choosing the place where to land the ship, fixing it with the instruments on board, and kept in orbit over the planet until, in that part of it, night fell.

CHAPTER XI

Zholta was afraid.

For the first time in a long time in years, Zholta knew he was going to die, and he was trembling.

His death would be horrible.

She didn't understand the reason for all this, but it had to be like that, and it would be like that, because they wanted it that way.

She was waiting, sitting on the hard floor of the cave, barely covered with a kind of tunic made from pieces of liana and leaves of certain kinds of trees, and with her hands tied behind her back.

And it would occur when the second of the three moons that illuminated the planet reached its zenith.

They did not understand her, and therefore there was no reason to explain things to them.

That would only serve to further aggravate their situation.

Zholta closed his eyes; I knew they would be here soon.

It was like this.

The skin covering the cave entrance was pushed aside and, somewhat startled, Zholta opened her eyes and looked at them.

There were five of them, but outside there were more.

They were the components of the Assyrian people, billions of years old.

The descendants of those others who first inhabited the planet.

"Stand up.

Zholta did it, laboriously, still looking at them facing the older of them.

With a long beard, the same as the others, with powerful muscles, very prominent cheekbones, strong and short legs, and inordinately long arms with a flattened nose, and a head, on the whole, completely square, except for the nape, which was elongated a little towards the back.

"Do you have something to say?

Zholta looked at them once more.

Almost covered with hair, in some places long and thick, curly, as if it were bristles, and barely covered ..., like the beings that populated a planet called Earth, billions of years ago.

It was, as if, suddenly, the past came fully alive to that Land of which the Assyrians had not the faintest idea.

Neither did Zholta.

Although it was different, in all respects

"Any.

"Do you know what the penalty is

"Yes, but I am not afraid.

He took a step toward the mouth of the cave.
"Waiting.
"What for, Kerr? It leads nowhere.
"I do not know yet.
Zholta took another step forward.
Outside, just a short distance away, Kelf was lowering the ship onto the planet.
"Waiting.
He stopped.
"For what? He repeated.
"You could try to make yourself understood.
"It's useless. I am different from you, and I have to disappear.
It was true, but there was something else, many more things, that had already been talked about, studied, discussed, to get nowhere.
It was different and was not understood.
Even when he spoke, his conversation or his words caused dread, even among the mightiest of Assyria.
The sorrow; to dead.
"It is true, Zholta. Let's go.
He did not respond, and began to walk.
Outside, the rocks, the moon, the stars shining in the black of the sky, the trees and the caves that housed the Assyrians.
All lit up, since around there were about a hundred, or perhaps more, of burning axes, from which the resin oozed.
Quite a funeral procession for Zholta, who shuddered when he saw them.
And silence, since no sound, even if it was inarticulate, emanated from those throats.
Only those corresponding to one sex, except for her, who was the opposite.
"Go.
He continued walking among the rocks, where his feet, completely barefoot, like those of the others, did not leave even the slightest trace, towards the esplanade surrounded by rocks with pointed edges.
A few minutes later, Zholta saw the pyre and the large rock filled with allegorical carvings depicting the adverse god of the Assyrians.
Topped off in a monstrous, repellent head.
They were going to sacrifice her there.
Zholta walked without taking a single misstep, climbed the small staircase that gave access to the pedestal that held the god, and remained like that, waiting for old Kerr to approach her, as he did.
He untied her hands and stripped her of her tunic.

Then he tossed it aside, somewhat away from the stone where he was going to tie it.

"Give me your hands, Zholta.

She did, and tied them again, but now in front of her body, and then a thick vine around her narrow bare waist, and thus tied her to the tall stone.

"Do you want something before we finish?

"Do not.

"Why?

"I read in your thinking.

"And what do you see?

"Treason.

Kerr convulsed, as if possessed by a fit of laughter, but his small eyes, almost sunk into their sockets, gleamed differently.

"To what and to whom?

"To Assyria, which is your people. You're old, Kerr, very old ... but still ... you still need me. One word from Zholta, and you would fight them for me, but Zholta won't utter it. "He closed his eyes and added," Go now, Kerr.

"Damn you...

He turned away.

The silence was grim.

The axes continued to illuminate the scene, ghostly, now stuck in the ground, forming a semicircle around the god and the victim they were going to sacrifice.

They did not speak.

But, silently, they piled dry branches and logs around the pedestal where Zholta stood.

They were going to burn it.

A single word, and maybe ... but Zholta would never say it.

* * *

Kelf saw the procession half an hour after they left the interside ship.

There was an atmosphere, and the planet's gravity was similar to the one he had abandoned six thousand light years ago, but despite this, perhaps because of the custom of other flights, he had put on the spacesuit, not the bell jar.

The cosmic ray gun glowed in his hand.

Five hundred loads, and none had been used.

Lights in the distance, moving, giving the impression of being a torch-lit procession ..., as if someone were preparing one of those famous voodoo dances of the 19th or early 20th century, on planet Earth.

Kelf stopped in his tracks, hesitated for a few seconds and continued walking, slowly, completely crouched among the rocks and undergrowth, following them now,
The esplanade.
Behind a small rocky massif he hid, violently astonished at the picture that was beginning to unfold before his eyes, as unexpected as it was incredible.
Two beings of the opposite sex, followed by others, in a funeral procession.
The robe on the ground, and she, completely motionless, on the rock pedestal.
Kelf lightly touched the trigger spring of his pistol.
But could he eliminate them like this, like this?
Yes, but he shouldn't.
Perhaps it was the reason for the large group that ...
They were going to burn her alive!
Kelf grimaced, and looked at them.
They were talking.
He could not hear the words, but those beings, like the first inhabitants of Earth, understood each other, and not precisely by gestures.
Now he was moving away from her.
Old, very old, ape-like.
Kelf raised the gun, but didn't fire.
I still couldn't.
Meanwhile, the wood pyre was growing near her feet.
It was blonde.
His body, dark, shone in the light of the torches and the moon, of the three moons that illuminated that planet, as if it had its own light.
Small, round and firm breasts, as he liked, firm hips and long thighs, ending in the perfect knee, which was followed by the shapely calf and small, bare, bare feet.
It was beautiful.
Kelf told himself he had to do something.
The torches were moving toward her now, and a murmur rose from the night, growing and growing.
Those madmen were going to set fire to the pyre.
It was then that Kelf pulled the trigger, but did not aim at the group.
The bolt made a terrifying hiss, snaked between the torches, and a rock weighing several tons some fifty yards to the right of the group flared into a blue-orange flare, exploded, and disappeared.
The torches froze, and the murmur stopped completely.
Kelf waited three more seconds, and pulled the trigger.

An ancient tree exploded in the night, illuminating the painting that was being represented, and it melted into the night, in less than a fifth of a second.

It was at that moment that he let himself be seen, driven by an idea that had just occurred to him at that moment.

He began to walk towards them, step by step, the barrel of the gun at hip level, and his strange white suit did what the cosmic rays could not.

The rout.

He heard them screaming, terrified, the torches fell to the ground, and their hasty steps were quickly lost in the night, among the boulders and the heaths that infected the surroundings.

Kelf quickened his pace, and suddenly he was in front of her eyes.

Black, impassive, as if what he was witnessing did not surprise him or was not afraid.

"Who are you?

"Zholta.

"What are you doing here?

"They were going to sacrifice me to Asiris. He is the god of their people.

"You are different.

"I know" he paused, and was surprised to add "You ... you come from the stars.

Kelf lost a few seconds of time, before answering:

"How do you know?

The large black eyes slid away from his, and he saw her gaze up at the sky.

"I talk to them" he said simply.

Kelf didn't reply. He cut through the vines that held her to the tall stone, then yanked her away.

Then he bent down, picked up the robe, and handed it to her.

"Cover yourself" he said.

He saw her smile.

"Why did they want to kill you?

"They do not understand me.

"Is it a motive?

"Yes.

He was tying his tunic around his narrow waist, still staring at her intently.

"You're scared of me?

"Do not.

The lost formula, the secret rué had accompanied him for ...

It was then that he inquired:

"You come with me?

"To the stars?

And he widened his eyes.
"Yes, that's right," Kelf replied.
A son, she could do it, his biological composition was the same as hers, his reproduction too.
He thought of Kronos, and marveled that at that moment there was no hatred for him, or for Alvia, who would have already passed away.
Yes, it had ceased to exist for millennia.
However, Kronos would still endure.
It was the Law of Life and Death.
He reached out his hand, and took one of his own.
"Come" he said.
They began to walk, silently, close together, among rocks, dirt, dust, and brush.
"How did you come to this place?
He saw her shrug.
"I do not know.
"What do you mean?
"My race lives on the other side of the planet, where now there is sun ... I ... I always saw these surroundings, so I think some of them brought me when I was very little.
"How did you not try the return?
"It was impossible. Even now it is. . If you don't take me on that thing that brought you here from the stars.
"Do you want me to?
"Do not. But I want to disappear from this planet. I will go with you. Zholta does not understand life or death. Nor does she understand that they want to kill her or that they kill each other. Zholta just wants peace and quiet. That is why he wishes to leave this planet "she cocked her head to look at him, and continued slowly": Zholta will give you children, Kelf.
He stopped short, releasing her hand, and faced her openly.
"How do you know all that?
"I read in minds. It's a gift, Kelf. So when I saw you, I knew that you came from the stars ... and that there is a Kronos and an Alvia. Who were they?
Without answering her question, he replied with another:
"Telepath?
Zholta's eyes widened.
"What's that? "He inquired." I don't understand you, Kelf.
"What you read in your mind" he commented
"Is it called that ...? Well, it is true. That is why they laugh to kill me. I know, of each one, everything bad and good that he holds within himself.
"It's a bonus," Kelf murmured, grabbing her hand again, and tugging at her.

Zholta replied again, replying:
"And upset. It takes away trust in others, and that makes Zholta always find herself alone. Who is Alvia?
"He has already died. Thousands of light years ago it died.
Once again he saw her surprise.
"I don't understand what you are trying to tell me.
"I will explain it to you over time, Zholta ... because I am going to give you something that I only possess within the Cosmos. Or at least, that's what I think.
"What is...?
She looked like a child, or perhaps she was, in some ways, from the way she asked the questions, from her curiosity, and Kelf tried to close her mind to that other one, perhaps much more powerful than her owner might suspect.
"I'll tell you on the ship" he replied.
Zholta did not reply, because at that moment the stone perhaps thrown by means of a sling or its equivalent reached her.
Kelf heard her moan, saw her turn around and fall to the ground like a sack, and immediately had to launch himself, as a shower of rocks began to fall around him.
The Assyrians, after the first moment of panic, and seeing their frustrated victim being carried away, attacked them in the only way they knew how.
Kelf crawled over to her, who was standing perfectly still on the grass, and stopped as soon as he reached her side.
Then, looking back, he saw them.
Not to all, but yes to some.
It could remove laughs in seconds, but it didn't.
The idea disgusted him.
They did what they believed was fair ... and not compelled by Kronos or the President of the Planet.
He fired twice, and the rocks that covered them vanished in sparks and pungent smoke. For the second time, he saw them running through the bushes, trees and rocks, and screaming, once again possessed by the demon of fear.
Kelf wasted no time, he took Zholta in his arms and ran with her, without dropping the weapon.
The ship.
He climbed the ladder, and stepped inside, his lungs on the verge of exploding, and laid her on the bunk.
He craved company. He had needed it for hours, centuries, and millennia, and now he had it.

He turned round, and closed the access door to the intersideral ship, knowing that at the time scheduled in advance, it would pick up the ladder and launch into space, to once again take the planned course, also in advance, in a journey that seemed to have no end.
Kelf returned to Zholta's side.
On the beautiful head, covered by long blond hair, there was blood.
He proceeded to examine her, knowing it was only a temporary loss of consciousness due to the stone, and then healed her with expert hands.
Than it really was.
Outside, against the hull of the ship, the thumps were louder and louder.
They were attacking them.
Kelf didn't move.
He did not care.
Even if they had other much more modern weaponry, they would not make a dent in that powerful hull incapable of melting even by the most frightening frictions, when entering or simply crossing through an atmosphere.
When Zholta recovered from his swoon, he saw the stars riding through space, at incredible speed backwards.
Zholta, fascinated by a spectacle she was seeing for the first time, approached one of the panels and for a long time, she was watching it, until suddenly, she turned away from there and looked for Kelf throughout the ship.
She wanted to ask him where they were going, led, more than anything else, by her natural curiosity about everything she saw. Found it in the lab.

* * *

"You haven't eaten in a long time, Kelf.
He looked at her.
She was beautiful, very beautiful, but he hadn't kissed her yet.
He thought about that, but what he replied was:
"Yes that's how it is.
"Come on, come with me.
It was getting closer to him.
How long had he been locked up?
Zholta asked himself the question as he got closer, unable to give himself a concrete answer.
Days, months or centuries; for her, time had also stopped counting.

Removing jars, comparing figures and more figures, torn papers on the floor, full of incomprehensible numbers, with eyes and face full of fatigue; eyes that were staring at her now, very intently.

"Go away, Zholta 'heard him say', this' is almost over, and I do not wish to delay it any longer.

"What is it?

Kelf forced a smile.

"You read in the mind.

"But not yours, Kelf. You closed it to me.

"And you do not like it?

"I do not count, since your will is mine.

"In that case, go, you understand?

Kelf thought.

Two ship stops ... and he had to find a world for Zholta. A world for both of us; it was essential that it should be so.

Two stops, and the journey that would never end ... but Zholta would already be dead when that happened, and he didn't want it.

She would not leave, she continued to approach him, with an expression in her eyes that he had never seen before.

He was circling the table behind which he stood, and now he was putting his hands on her shoulders, leaning more, more and more.

"I'm going to give you children, Kelf" he whispered. It is your will and mine, do you understand?

And crushed them; lips against hers.

The hug lasted a long time, maybe hours, and time was pressing, so Kelf had to push her away, almost slapping her, and, without wanting to see her surprise gesture, he said:

"We are wasting time, Zholta.

"And you do not like it?

"Yes, but we must not. Not for now. Go and wait for me. Ah! Turn on the screen. You will see, with your eyes, things that you will be interested to know ... and that I cannot explain to you.

He kissed her once more, and, at last, he saw himself alone, in front of the flasks in the ship's laboratory, and the numbers that for months he had tried to piece together,

Now, everything was finished.

He was going to give Zholta all his power, and then… he would burn all those papers again, all those formulas that had been a secret for millennia, even to Kronos himself.

Ideas ...

That they could not be had on the Planet because Kronos forbade them.

Bah!
Zholta was in front of the screen when he approached, holding a long tube
of orange liquor.
"Drink," he said.
Surprised, she looked into his eyes, then reached out and took it.
"It's… what I saw on the screen, right?
"Yes that's how it is.
Zholta drank.

CHAPTER XII

He was startled, as soon as he woke up.
Nothing was happening inside the ship, but he knew something had changed. It was his intuition, the so-called sixth sense that warned him, and Kelf got to his feet.
Beside him, Zholta slept peacefully.
Around him the ship continued its journey, but there was something else; something I did not understand.
They did not seem to move, or even move, which was not unusual in space, but there was a vague feeling that they were just floating, as if adrift.
Kelf dressed and ran to one of the panels, which he opened to look.
Blacks
He went to the other, pacing the ship from one end to the other, with strange haste, and carried out the same operation.
Blackness, without a single bright point, to indicate the location of the stars, simply because there were none.
He ran his hands over his eyes, but that, the horrible sight, persisted.
There were no stars anywhere, the ship had crossed the wall that divided the confines of the Universe, and had entered nothingness, following its inexorable march.
Two stops ... and one of them would be to backtrack for twenty-four hours ... which would be useless, since the intersidership's autopilot would return to the course it was now heading.
Kelf stepped away from the panel and flopped down on the first thing he found, and that's how Zholta found him, an hour later.
From that moment on, neither of them knew how much time passed, but it was centuries, during which they sailed, or at least they believed so, through that black mass, which seemed to have absorbed them forever.
It was one morning, Kelf believed, when, in the distance, in front of the ship, he saw the first bright spots.
"Zholta" almost screamed. " Check it out.
She ran to his side, and for a long time they watched them until they began to circle the ship.
“They are… they are stars, Kelf, worlds that move. Now I will give you the children I denied you, when we get into that horror, Kelf.
He did not respond, he looked, and as he did and as time passed, his pulse quickened because something was happening there that he never suspected.
Something much more incredible than everything they had left behind!
The stars, the constellations, the nebulae ...
Kelf passed his hand across his forehead, and closed his eyes.

The image persisted ... and the ship continued its inexorable march, without being able to stop it.

They were going to pass by and Zholta ...

No, such an event would not occur.

Kelf knew it days later when, in front of his eyes, the yellow light began to shine, and he did not wait another second.

He took the controls and, without saying a word, while your Zholta stood silently by his side, watching him, setting the course.

Hours that lasted a long time or maybe weeks in his own judgment, although he knew that couldn't be since he only had twenty-four, when the point in front of the ship began to grow and grow.

The clouds, the deserts, the valleys, the hills, the lakes and the continents came.

"Will we descend?

"Yes.

Kelf's voice was hoarse, and his forehead was perspiring.

"What star is that?

"The Planet, Zholta. The earth. Mother of the Galaxy I

And not even he himself understood, until much later, the meaning of his own words.

He entered the Earth's atmosphere, with only one idea in mind, that of descending as soon as possible on the surface of the Planet, but he did choose at random, an area in shadows, near the Great City, on its outskirts.

Kelf wanted to find out something.

On the ground, he turned to look at her.

"Can you handle the ship? "I ask.

"You showed me.

"I have to find out something, and it will take a couple of hours" he continued explaining. You are going to stay, do you understand? They don't dress like you, and I don't want you to attract attention. But if it doesn't come back for any other reason, you will leave Earth, with no help other than that of the ship ... and you will not be able to stop more than once. Do it ... with yours, on your distant Planet, Zholta. But look closely at one thing, that light will only turn on once ... and you should not touch the controls, when this happens. Let the ship navigate alone, as if nothing had happened, do you understand?

"Yes.

"Then, wait for it to turn on again, and then ... find your planet.

"But...

He didn't wait, and Kelf left the ship

The suburb.

It was then that he stopped in his tracks and froze, because that was just unbelievable.
They were there, almost in front of him, in one of the corners, their backs turned.
Two Robot-Beings.
Two Kronos Robots.
Kelf put his hands to his eyes and rubbed them furiously.
When he finished, he looked.
There was no mistake.
He took one step, another, hesitating, as a horrible suspicion began to grip his mind, and he stopped.
In front of him, the Robot-Beings did not move.
Of vigilance...?
The idea.
It was horrible.
Kelf began to back away.
I was at the same starting point.
It was as if nothing had happened ... but what had to happen.
He had taken off from the City on a journey of millennia, thousands of light years, and was at the same destination ... where everything was exactly the same.
Wide-eyed, a look of madness on his face, he started backing away step by step.
Alvia and Kelf ...
Volmen and Frida.
He remembered when the blackness swallowed up the ship on that horrifying summit The stars, without a single point of light. He had reached the ends of the Universe, he had crossed them between a milky mass of blackness ... and that black peak that for light years he crossed had served as a bridge, as a funnel tunnel to break the barriers of Space-Time, retreating in the Passed up to its time
It was ... incomprehensible, but it happened.
He had traveled towards the Future for thousands of light years, since they made him take off from Earth, expelled from Kronos, to go back to the Past, also breaking all the laws that supported Space-Time.
It made its own Epoch, where everything ... would continue the same.
He did not even know now if the ship with Zholta would continue behind him, if that one would have returned to its Time ... if he, when walking towards the Great City, headquarters of Kronos, of the President, of the Great Council, had broken those barriers ... after tracing an orbit of madness, for that.

With drunken steps, knowing that, if he stayed, that if he entered the Great City, despite knowing the facts, he could not prevent them from repeating themselves, since the course of History could not be changed, he continued to retreat into the shadows, trembling, his face contorted, towards the interstellar ship, not knowing, as he already thought, if it had returned to the Future.

Kelf was lucky.

It took Zholta hours, days and months to get back to the reality of the moment.

It was that night, hugging him, when she whispered in his ear:

"We will return to my Planet Kelf, with my people ... and I will have those children that I desire.

"Yes, whatever you want, Zholta" he replied, kissing her. We will return to your time.

She opened her eyes a lot.

"My time...? I don't understand you, Kelf.

He closed his eyes, hiding his head against her sturdy shoulder.

"One day ... I'll explain it to you ..., but he's not longing. Not now.

I would ... but it was horrible ...

Alvia and Kelf.

Alvia and himself.

A jump back in the Cosmos ... and everything was the same.

END